UNVEILED

Unveiled

Mountain Warriors Book 5

R.J. BURLE

Pier House Books

DEDICATION

To Brian Adams (not the singer) A very wise man who taught me very much and I am ever grateful for him. I had the honor of exchanging books with him that we each have written.

PROLOGUE

Douglas Bircher scrambled a mad stumbling dash up the rocky incline, leaving a smear of his blood on a small patch of snow in the expansive leaf litter from a ragged gunshot wound on his thigh.

"It's just a leg wound," he tried to tell himself, but he didn't have the luxury to check it, and he knew from experience that a person could bleed to death if not treated.

His breath was as ragged as the wound and his pounding heartbeat crashed louder in his ears than the thick crunch of brown oak leaves beneath his boots. Occasionally he winced as gunfire erupted from the forest behind him. As he ran, bark from a nearby tree blasted in his face from a bullet's impact. That tree could have been his chest.

He pushed himself a further five meters up the steep hill and dove behind a small boulder protruding from the ground like a defiant fist at the sky. Immediately he heard bullets slapping the rock and the crack of angry gunshots in the distance.

Peeking over the rock, Douglas saw vague shapes of his hunters running after him in the growing twilight. He hastily aimed his handgun over his cover and fired in the general direction of one of his pursuers, and was rewarded with the satisfying recoil and report, but he missed as his target dove to the ground.

He carefully aimed at another man in the far distance who was still standing. The man's face filled his gun sites. Douglas squeezed the trigger again. Nothing happened, not even an impotent click. He had lost count but knew he was out of ammo. That last round that he fired would keep his pursuers at bay at most for a minute if they didn't already realize that he was out of bullets.

He knew that he should have made his final bullet count, but he had to stop his pursuers from surrounding him. That last shot gave him a temporary reprieve of a few minutes at the most. But when his life was measured in seconds, minutes seemed like an extravagant luxury.

He cursed as he placed the empty handgun into his pants and pulled out a bowie knife. Then he changed his mind and pulled his handgun back out. With the mind crushing terror of his armed pursuit, it was hard to formulate a plan. He held the gun in his left hand and blade in his right. It may be empty but if he aimed it at his hunters, they would hopefully pause more than they would if he pointed or even threw his knife at them. Most of the time, pointing an unloaded firearm at armed pursuers was suicidal, but these guys weren't going to take him prisoner. Douglas was keen on purchasing his life by the fraction of a second in this mess that he'd gotten himself into and making a spur of the moment plan in the next second.

He twisted to move up the hill and cursed savagely as he looked down at his pant leg. He hadn't had a chance to look at the wound yet on the outside of his upper thigh. A ragged, glossy gash from his blood flow marred his black paramilitary trousers. Some scarlet drops leaked from the denim into the detritus of the forest floor. He couldn't see the wound well through the bullet hole in his pant leg but knew it wasn't life threatening. That is, it wouldn't have been life threatening if he could hole up and rest for a week or so, but that was obviously a wealth far beyond his current means. There was no med-evac in a helicopter in this war. In fact a helicopter crew was likely to target him. However he wasn't sure how much further he could run losing his life blood at a slow but steady flow.

Douglas had been wandering the Forbidden Zone alone for the last week, a very horrible predicament for anyone to find himself in but as someone in exile, he had no choice. It started when the ultimate authority in the Forbidden Zone, The Specter, a man who wore a realistic skull-faced mask, was given charge of him and three other soldiers from Craigsvill who were led to the Cavern of the Vampires to be offered as food for the vamps and a hideous monstrosity called The Mind. The Mind was a twenty foot tall humanoid that was able to tap into the electric impulses of computers and the neurons of people.

Douglas didn't understand exactly what he had witnessed, but someone or a few someones had taken over the control of his mind and his very will as well as the minds of his fellow soldiers. Three of them, all hardened fighting men, stood still and helpless as the fourth soldier was drained of blood by the vampires and then flung to The Mind, who ate him crunching on the bones and all. The remaining soldiers including himself were frozen in place by some form of psychic control. Douglas shuddered as he could still hear the monster crunching on his friend's bones as the vampires drank his blood from a communal chalice. The dead man was named Sam, and through the bonds of battle, Sam had been like a brother to Douglas.

Douglas Bircher would have died too, but a vampiress named Abigail helped him escape and gave him the handgun as well as a fresh killed squirrel to eat after she drained it of blood, of course. She made him promise not to return to Craigsville for fear that under torture he would betray her.

Owing her his life and fearful of the repercussions that he would face from both Craig and The Specter if he returned to Craigsville, he conceded to her wishes. However, two years of living in a post apocalypse world had turned the survivors in the land as savagely territorial as guard dogs. Anyone wandering into a group's territory was seen with suspicion. First it was pondered what atrocity the wanderer committed to earn an exile from the safety of their prior home. Second, refugees were either a new person to take scarce food from the mouths of their already starving children or a potential raider who would kill their children. Lastly, everyone had witnessed a healthy outsider welcomed into their communities suddenly turn into a zombie from a bite they kept hidden, and once turned, the guest would attack. These days, compassion and hospitality were seen as the virtues of the foolish as well as the dead.

In Douglas' case, today, he had simply been caught with a deer that he had killed in one tribe's unmarked territory. Surrounded by a band of ten angry, armed men, as he stood over the dead deer, Douglas sarcastically apologized for not having psychic powers to read that he intruded on their neck of the woods.

Despite a ravaging hunger, Douglas would have been happy to walk away and leave the deer to the offended tribe, but the patriarch of the ten men, a severely sharp featured, gray bearded man attempted to reach for the handgun at Douglas' hip. Due to his prior training in law enforcement and the War on Terror, not to mention surviving the ravages of the post apocalypse Forbidden Zone for two years in Craigsville's security force, Douglas responded instinctively and violently. He shot the old man perfectly in the center of the chest and he immediately shot another man who also reached for him.

After he shot the gray beard, one of the ten men cried, "Father!"

Douglas cringed, both in sympathy for the son and worry for himself. He knew the adult son would pursue him relentlessly to eithers' death.

With only a handful of bullets left in his handgun, Douglas dashed into some leafy rhododendrons and disappeared followed by a hail of bullets that miraculously missed him until that one grazed his leg.

His pursuers had spread out behind him and dragnetted his trail. He heard one yelp in triumph when he found Douglas' blood trail. Had they not spotted the blood, they may have given up as night approached, but with the knowledge that he was injured, they began the running battle over the last hour.

Now he pressed himself to the ground behind his cover as a hail of gunfire hammered the rocks, trees and dirt around him. The fragments of rock and wood from the assault of bullets peppered his face and body.

Douglas looked for his next place to run and determined his plan. Up above him, some fifty yards, just beneath the ridgeline's summit, he spotted another rock outcropping that would give him cover. More importantly, it would give him a clear view of the valley and those who were stalking him. If he had more ammunition he could have held them off from that vantage point until night, and probably easily killed all of them or simply slipped away in the cover of darkness on the other side of the ridge. He nervously looked at the cloudy sky and guessed that he had thirty minutes to nightfall.

However his goal now would be to simply bluff them that he had endless magazines of bullets and once he made the vantage point, he would shout at them that from the kindness of his heart he'd let them go to take care of the two men who he had shot so that they might live. Because the outcropping was close to a ridge top, he hoped that during the bluff, he could sneak and make his escape into the opposite valley as darkness fell. Although it was dangerous to wander a woods during the night that was stalked by zombies and vampires, they weren't his immediate threat. Although zombies and vampires were attracted by gunfire due to the promise of a wounded meal, he feared his fellow survivors more than the monsters.

Douglas flinched as a ripping pain shot up from the wounded leg when he twisted it slightly to get to his feet. He gnashed his teeth. With the adrenaline induced numbness wearing off, he was now feeling the pain rather than the initial shock of the bullet wound. His leg was also stiffening.

In his condition it would be better to avoid any fight. Hell, he thought, it would be a miracle if he simply made it to that rock outcropping without acquiring another wound.

Another staccato of bullets peppered the ground around him and he knew that the gun fire was intended for him to keep his head down as cover for the others in the hunting party to rush his position or get into cover for a clearer shot at Douglas from an exposed flank on higher ground. Douglas had to move.

As soon as the gunfire ceased Douglas took a deep breath as if preparing to dive underwater, shot up to his feet, and sprinted unevenly to a thick poplar tree above him. He dove behind it and stood up. Leaning against the trunk on the safe side, he could feel the violent shaking of the rounds that slammed into his protection through the wood. As soon as that fusillade ended he sprinted to another tree up the hill. He almost fell as his foot, slick with blood, kept slipping with squishing noises on the insole inside of his boot. He sighed as he realized that the leg wound was worse than he suspected, especially if he was both leaving a bloodtrail that they could follow as well as filling his boot. Douglas took a moment behind the cover and tied his boot as tight as he could to try to minimize the slippage.

Next, he looked above for different positions to gain cover on his mad sprint to the outcropping at the top of the ridge. He figured he would need at least three thick tree trunks or boulders to hide behind between his current position and his goal. Three wild sprints. If he was in the open too long, they'd surely get him.

Once again bullets slammed into the thick poplar tree causing him to flinch, interrupting his study of the path. When he opened his eyes again, he came to the realization that between the lack of cover and his waning energy from steady blood loss, one final zigzag sprint for the cover at the top was his best option. Sometimes a moving target was hard for even a seasoned warrior, especially when it came to killing another man. He prayed that his attackers weren't psychopaths and that deep down they'd unconsciously hesitate even for a split second to draw bead on another person, especially on the back of a fleeing man.

He caught himself bending over and holding his breath as if readying himself to sprint into a heavy thunderstorm of lead from one shelter to another. A hell of a downpour he thought with irony.

He removed the black cap of his uniform and waved it outside of his cover. Instantly the guns below him thundered and blazed with rage. He waited for the responding fire to die down, figuring that when the barrage ended, his hunters would either be reloading or reevaluating their positions after moving in closer under the covering fire. He flinched as he heard another barrage of lead peppering his tree. The explosive fire of the guns was closer than before.

He peeked below and saw three men rushing to a position within fifty meters. Anger burned in their eyes, fueled by the death of their leader. Douglas also knew that they wanted to finish killing him before darkness settled. These last few minutes before sunset would be their final rush. There would be no mercy for him.

A silence reigned for a minute. As soon as another coordinated salvo began to cover those rushing he steeled himself for his own rush uphill. He would make a mad sprint for the top. He had to.

A quiet moment passed, and he sprinted straight up the hill again almost slipping on the blood between the soaked sock and insole of his boot as well as loose rocks and other debris, but he powered on as the fresh adrenaline pounded and pumped into his arteries. As soon as the gunfire erupted below he zigged to the right.

In his time in the military, one of the more basic things that was drilled into him was that when charging an enemy line or retreating, you'd say to yourself, "I'm up! He sees me! I'm down!" Upon saying, "I'm down," he was supposed to drop to the ground and roll to a different position of cover or concealment, and repeat the process as many times as needed to get to his goal.

Instead, he powered up the steep slope repeating the combat mantra. When he'd tell himself, "I'm down," he'd zigzag back and forth up the hill, as bullets kicked up leaves and rocks around him. So far the bullets were just barely missing him. The enemy fired and aimed with no hesitation and no regret. They wanted him dead and they were almost deadly accurate. Almost, either that or Douglas had been most fortunate, so far.

He kept pushing his tired legs up the hill that was so steep that occasionally he would use his hands to scramble on all fours and pull himself up on the exposed tree roots and the trunks of saplings.

When he was within fifteen yards of the rock outcropping, he stumbled and rolled to his right as bullets slammed into the space he had just occupied moments before. He was in the open and jolted to his hands and knees and quick crawled up a steep section to a relatively flat spot. His legs powered him to stand and sprint the last few yards. He was thinking he was almost home free when he was slammed to the ground. It felt like someone had kicked his boot out from under him. He realized that a bullet had destroyed the heel of his boot. Although the lead round didn't hit his body, the impact was so shocking that it knocked him off his feet. Without hesitation, he propelled himself up and dove and rolled the final three yards up and over the rock outcropping ignoring the pointed stones that dug into his body as he hit the ground.

He swore as he landed in front of the scuffed military black boots of a black clad man armed with an M-16. One of the pursuers must have come up from an alternate route to flank him. Douglas caught a flash of the man's face in the setting sun and thought he looked familiar, but didn't have time to dwell on it. Douglas rolled to the side hoping he was quick enough before the man with the M-16 could draw a bead on him.

He cringed as the gunfire erupted inches above his head.

| 1 |

That night I stood strong on the top of a cliff, the blood of enemies stained my sword, face, and body. I feared nothing, not even the dark despite owning the full knowledge of what lurked in its shadows. I was no longer Eric Hildebrande, the journalist. I had outlived all expectations. I not only survived a few days chased by vampires in their seemingly endless home caverns, but I slayed a great number of them in the process of my escape.

I had just thrown the head of David, the giant vampire, off the cliff. I screamed war cries into the night over and over across the dark abyss created by the precipice. My voice finally went hoarse. It was only when my throat refused to scream that I stopped and I leaned against the trunk of the great oak to rest. But my mind couldn't rest.

I was insane. It wasn't that I lost my mind, but it had been taken from me. I hoped it was temporary, but the fire that raged inside of me felt unquenchable. I wanted to kill something, anything.

Before his death, David had psychically imprinted the chant of "Kill! Kill! Kill!" in my head. It repeated without cessation even after his death. He had implanted it to get me to kill Richard the head vampire. Ironically, the mantra drove me to kill David instead of Richard.

Along with his chant, I was covered in David's vampiric blood. The vampiress, Abigail, had warned me that when human skin contacts vampiric blood, it conjures a burning insanity. A person's psionic perceptions are increased and the increased input of foreign thoughts in one's mind becomes overwhelming. You can't tell your own mind from the minds of others. The person's immune system heightens to fight the vampiric viral infection and it causes a rage in the person's deepest fiber. That was no joke. My mind felt as if it was savagely hacked to pieces, reassembled and sliced again over and over. The contact with the blood also caused needle-like pain all over my body, particularly my face that was coated in its drying wetness.

I fingered the bark of the great oak tree that I leaned on for support. It was the same one that stopped my plummet down the precipice on my first night in the Forbidden Zone over a week ago. The tree had bruised my face, nearly shattering my nose, but it saved my life from a fall down the cliff.

I heard something walking toward me in the dry leaf litter, but I didn't flinch. I was prepared to kill any enemy or die trying. I really didn't care which one it was at this moment of insanity. I raised my blade in the direction of the sound. I realized that David's psychic command to kill Richard was now screaming even louder "Kill! Kill! Kill!" I had grown used to it and accepted it with the rage that shot through me. A part of me worried that the insanity and the chant to kill would forever be embedded in my mind. Another section of myself relished the mad feeling of power coursing through my blood.

I wanted to kill them all. David was controlling me beyond the grave. I wanted to kill him again. I wanted to, "kill, kill, kill!" I knew I was insane. I needed help.

I saw the black hooded figure of a vampire. It kept approaching me, unafraid of my blade. I steeled myself to deliver death, but then, I relaxed just a bit. Despite its dark appearance of impending doom, the creature didn't seem threatening.

"Abigail?" I asked, only lowering my blade in the slightest. I felt a degree of sanity and relief wash over me. Just a small degree, but it was a great relief.

"Yes, Eric, it's me," she said in a tired voice. I could hear the strain from the shattered rib cage and lung wound received when we killed The Mind together. The twenty foot tall, monstrous being had gripped her body in its gigantic hand and crushed her. If she had been a human rather than a vampire, she would have died instantly. She would probably recover in a few days, but she needed time to mend. Vampiric "immortality" had limits.

Abigail smiled at me with a hint of concern for my well being, but the graciousness in her smile melted my fiery heart. I lowered my sword all the way so that the point hovered an inch off the ground. Bryan, the warchief of the Mountain Warriors, had instilled in me never to let the blade touch the ground, both out of respect for the sword and so as not to dull the blade by accidentally dashing it against a stone. I now had an uncanny instinct as to the nearness of the uneven ground to my steel.

Abigail walked up, stood beside me and we stared together over the precipice.

"I saw you sleeping here your first night," she said.

"That night, I thought--" I began. "You protected me from that bear, didn't you?"

"You thought you were seeing things," she finished.

"But you didn't kill me..."

She shook her head. "I could tell you had a good heart."

"I fooled you," I joked but didn't smile.

I felt bad for not truly seeing her for who she really was all this time. All through our time together beneath the Caverns of the Vampires, I worried that she would attempt to kill me or turn me into a vampire. She had been ordered to do so under the threat of death. Instead, she helped me escape, not to mention killed dozens of other vampires while at my side in the process.

"May I lean on you," she asked as she looked up at me. I felt like I could swim in the clear, welcoming pools of her eyes.

"Of course," I said as I opened an arm to invite the vampire into my confidence.

When she leaned into me, I could feel in her flinching structure how she suffered from her injury. I wrapped my arm around her. I wanted to melt into her as my heart had just seemed to melt in my chest at the sound of her sweet, melodic voice.

"Easy with the ribs. They should be mended in a day or two, but they hurt right now," she said with a brave smile to mask her pain.

She snuggled into my chest as I pulled her slightly tighter about the waist, avoiding her ribcage. The top of her head was at my nose level and the pheromones in her hair tantalized my nostrils and drove me crazy. A distant part of my brain wondered if the madness induced by the blood of the vampires fired up my passions for lust as well as my rage. David's "Kill. Kill. Kill," was but a whisper now.

She smelled my chest and said, "You need not hide your human scent from me. I enjoy it, and not for your blood either," she said with a slightly suggestive smile as she looked up at me, but her statement was filled more with genuine affection than a flirtatious game. She was in far too much pain for that. She looked down and nuzzled my chest again.

"Killing The Mind didn't kill the failed vampires," I said with disappointment.

The Mind could telepathically link to the electromagnetic fields of both computers and human neurons. He had controlled most of the vampires. Surprisingly, Abigail had a degree of immunity from him. We thought that killing The Mind would kill the vampires under its control, but instead they only seemed slightly dazed for a moment. I felt like we failed in our mission.

She replied, "There are other Minds in this area. They filled in the gap, but let's savor our small victory for the present."

"Yes," I agreed.

The words, I love you, hovered on the tip of my tongue as I nestled my face against the soft hair on the top of her head. I didn't sense her mind probing mine, but I could tell that she felt the same simply by the way she melted back into me. I moved my hand from her ribcage as I felt her cringe. I marveled again that any human would have died with what she suffered. What would take a month or more of healing for a person, a vampire could do in a few days without medical care. I also suspected that she was resilient without the vampiric virus. I had never met anyone like her.

With her head resting on my pectoral muscle and shoulder, she looked up at me again. Under the dismal night sky, her eyes brightened with their own natural light of passion. Her red lips were welcoming.

We looked at each other longer than such a moment should take before lips embrace in passionate intimacy. I had really wanted her, but we held back for just a moment. A moment that didn't happen.

"I never wish to leave your side," she said.

"Yes," I agreed, but as I stared at her in awe, my capability of speech had left me.

I loved her. At that moment, I suddenly felt victorious, but in retrospect, I failed. I forgot about rescuing Bradley, Bryan's young son, who was kidnapped by her coven. It was the sole purpose of entering the cave. However, it was the vampiress who saved him. It was Abigail who saved me, but I didn't know that she had saved the child at that moment. The maddening psychic game that had been played made me forget about Bradley after Abigail and I killed The Mind.

I looked down at her face as my lips hovered above hers.

"Abigail," I whispered.

"Eric," she whispered back.

She looked at me with the fathomless pools of her eyes. Her face was relaxed in a complete surrender to me and I felt my own will melt and become hers. I looked into her deep eyes and I felt like I was diving into an endless pool of pleasure. My entire being floated and I lost contact with reality. Mentally and then physically, she drew me into her as I stared into her eyes. She became my entire world. Everything else ceased to exist. Including me. There was only us. Abigail and me. Us. Nothing else. We were the universe. It was too magical to be real. We didn't kiss, but we were locked in this moment.

I literally felt as if my brain was getting sucked into her head and hers into mine. My face felt as if it was elongating as I was physically, yes, physically pulled into her. Something inside of me screamed. I realized I had no control. My mind felt psychically under her domination. It felt like my body had suddenly been transformed into plasticity to be psychically molded in the tendrils of her mind. I no longer stood above the cliff with her. Unfathomable darkness surrounded me as I spun out of control into an abysmal void. I literally wondered where and even who I was.

I could distantly feel myself freeze. I pulled back from her, and blinked, staring at her as if for the first time. Reality crashed into me with a physical-like impact. The blood on her face from the enemies we slew together glittered in the starlight.

"What's wrong?" she asked.

"You were just controlling me," I said, suddenly thoroughly confused.

"No, we were giving ourselves to each other mentally."

"You were controlling me," I said with what I felt was a clear mind.

"No, Eric. Vampires let themselves link their emotions with those whom they love," she said with innocence that I wasn't buying.

It suddenly dawned on me as I raged, "You made me forget Bradley!"

"Eric," she pleaded. I found out later and too late, that she had saved Bradley and had used her psychic powers to make me forget him. In retrospect, if I, a human, had followed her through the Caverns of the Vampires, I only would have hindered her rescue. Her decision was wise, but I was too maddened to see it at the moment. What I had just experienced, getting sucked into her mind, was so foreign and new, it sent my very being into panic. Not to mention the blood madness already affecting me.

I glared at her trying to recover my mind. Looking in her eyes I could see that she made me forget the boy who I was supposed to rescue. That's what inadvertently propelled me to seek David's and Richard's death so irrationally.

"Are you alright?" she asked, very concerned.

For a moment, I was afraid to give the answer. It felt as if a switch had suddenly been pulled, not just in my mind but in every cell, my soul, indeed, my very being. I felt as if a counter electric current flowed through me throwing every affectionate instinct that I had been feeling into full reverse. Fear and anger at that last violation suddenly replaced love and affection. Again I felt the stinging needles of vampiric blood on my skin. The same vampiric blood that flowed through her. Abigail and I were separate species.

"Are you alright?" she asked again.

When I didn't answer she cocked her head curiously, lips still invitingly pursed.

A vampiress' lips that were red with blood. A bite definitely transferred the vampiric virus, but I also suspected that a mere kiss on the lips could do the same.

David's command suddenly began to chant in my head again. No. The dead vampire was screaming in my head to, "Kill! Kill! Kill!" It now echoed loudly, overwhelming and breaking my mind again. Even though it was in my head, I wanted to cover my ears to silence that psychic voice. A surge of violent desire welled up inside of me to be unleashed on anything that I touched. Abigail!

In that rage of vampiric blood madness and David's chant, I violently pushed away what I suddenly saw as a monstrous beast enshrined in the fleshy costume of a beautiful woman.

I savagely snarled at her, "Go back to your brood, vampiress. My life from this point on will be devoted to killing all evil, starting with your kind, including you if we meet again."

"Eric..." she pleaded. "It's the blood madness. It's not you saying that."

"Shut up, witch!" I exclaimed with my blood splashed sword still in hand, raising it for battle.

She backed up and when she felt comfortable with the distance said, "Let me join you in this endeavor against evil."

"Kill! Kill! Kill!" I heard David's long dead voice screaming in my head. His final psychic command was in complete control of my passions and driving my instinct.

I glowered at her and took an aggressive step toward her.

"You would kill me with the sword that I gave you?" she asked. "A sword that has saved your life many times?"

"Yes! To ensure that I don't become an infected thing like the rest of you disease ridden parasites." I blurted out. My fight was against the remains of David, not her, but I couldn't see it. Madness consumed me like a flame.

She looked down as if hurt, and then she looked at me as her eyes flashed with anger. I felt the tendrils of her mind attempting to influence my own, to calm me, but it only enraged me more.

She said, "David still has his control embedded in you, Eric."

I looked at her and the vision flashed back and forth. One fraction of a second she had her fangs bared, eyes ablaze with the lust for my blood. In the next hair width of time her pleading eyes probed into my own. Her fangs hidden behind pursed lips. The visions flashed back and forth like a strobe light. I knew one wasn't real and the other might not be real either. I trusted nothing. I was going insane with the blood madness and the chant to kill. I wasn't seeing anything real. Just insanity.

One thing that I was kind of sure of was that she was attempting to reach into my mind to console me. Whether she meant well or not, I wanted no one in my head but me. With the mental overload, I almost sank to my knees and held my ears against David's chant to kill, but instead, I screamed a war cry and charged her. I swung my sword down to decapitate her, but she bent her neck submissively, and I barely stopped inches from slicing her. She offered no tricks or resistance. I shakily held my blade inches above her exposed neck, frozen to move forward or away.

I finally withdrew the sword to my side but didn't scabbard it.

She lifted her head and looked at me. Her eyes didn't hold fear, anger or submission, but only compassion. I was overwhelmed with tender feelingings for her and guilt that seem to light my veins on fire with more torture. I wanted it all to go away. I both wanted to curl up in a numbed fetal position as well as detonate and explode into flames and then into welcoming nothingness. I hated myself for what I almost did, but that just infuriated me more. I hated everything including myself, above all.

Abigail said, "I would sooner die by your blade, than to harm you in any way, Eric. You know that. It is the blood madness that you suffer now. I warned you. It will wear off as soon as you wash. Let me help you."

"But you would infect me with your diseased kiss!" The conflicting forces of instinctive passionate attraction versus the equally strong desire for self preservation against the vampiric infection waged a violent war inside that conflagrated into a violent anger. Not to mention the blood madness compounded with David's chant from beyond the grave to kill everything in sight. It threatened to consume the woman-like thing before me as well as myself.

"Eric," she pleaded. "I wasn't going to kiss you on the lips. I give you my word, I wish I could give myself to you fully, but I never would do anything to harm you. You know that. You know that. I went through this too when I contacted vampire blood. This is not you! I was trying to give myself mentally, not physically. Vampires mix our minds with those we truly care for."

I wanted to believe her, but the madness controlled me. That mind meld or whatever it was when I was sucked into her felt more like psychic control, than an intimate mixing of minds. I said to her, almost begging her, "Leave before I kill you. Please. I can't control myself. I will kill you next time I see you."

I could see fear, but mostly hurt in her eyes. I purposely cut off her access from my mind. She backed away, keeping a wary eye on me. She knew my threats to be true at this moment. I had to get away from the scene immediately before I said or did anything that I would regret even more than what I already said and did. To leave was the only true control of myself that I still retained.

I began to back away along the edge of the precipice aware of the cliff and rocky shards a hundred feet below, but becoming a vampire worried me more than a fall. A life where I fed on the blood of others and hid in shame from the sun was intolerable, and I could never hold love for anything that lived such a miserable existence. That's what I told myself. Although, conflictingly, I loved her. I swear to the heavens I loved her and that pain of not being able to be with her fired the rage in me more. Every bit of tenderness I felt for her, painfully raged in my veins and tortured my soul.

I finally turned and began the journey back to the village of the Mountain Warriors. My mind raged and roiled in the madness of battles between conflicting ideas as I walked. I still had that longing for Abigail, however any compassion, mercy, or love that I had for her was strictly based on irrational attraction for the opposite sex, I told and tried to convince myself. If David, the monstrous vampire who I slew earlier that night, had offered friendship and got in my mind as Abigail had just done, I would have struck him down with such violence as I already had.

But God, I still loved Abigail. She had saved me more than once. I wanted to believe what she told me, but I cast that from my mind. That feeling of getting sucked into her head in whatever that mind meld was was too much in my current state.

I now had to go face my village for their betrayal. They had abandoned me in the Caverns of the Vampires. If I had succumbed to the vampires, I would have returned to wreak my vengeance upon them as an undead. Now, I would just have my vengeance in human form. I realized that, in my temporary insanity, I not only wished to slay evil but everything in my path as well, including people. I worried that the madness was permanent, but I was out of control and at the mercy of the insanity induced by the blood of the vampires on my skin. It was so bad that I couldn't even conceptualize washing it off. I could only walk back to the village in a fuming rage.

Adam, the chief of the Mountain warriors, had ordered the retreat from the caverns. His power over me in the past was based on fear and respect. He was strong, cunning and wise. Now I had no fear of death. My only fear was not ridding the world of evil with blade or bullet and ridding it of anyone who stood in my way, whether they were innocent or not. The fear of what I was becoming angered me more. It was an endless downward spiral of rage. Every thought stabbed me physically and mentally.

In the past, mediocrity had been too lofty of a goal for me. Now, I was a different man. I ruled my own destiny, or so I told myself.

I followed a bear trail down the mountain. Critter, the tribe's tracker, had explained the difference between a human trail versus bear. The vegetation of animal trails tended to circle the path as if to hug the large crawling animal. That left the branches to angrily slap my face and chest as I stormed down the path. Even the crunch of the leaves beneath my boots infuriated me more. For some reason, I took this all as a personal affront. As if mother nature was purposefully trying to piss me off more.

Also bears tended to go from one food or water source to another such place. In the past, human trails tended to go to majestic overlooks and to inspiring peaks, but recent times had placed primitive needs over majestic summits. In short, the human hiking trails were slowly disappearing into the reclamation of the forest from lack of use. Sightseeing was a luxury that no one could afford these days. Now humans were taking over the bear trails and eating the animals that they ran into, or getting eaten by the bears.

This wasn't one of those trails where I had to worry about bears too much. It was high on the shoulders of Shining Rock Mountain and Cold Mountain and most of the hunting and food gathering happened far below in the valleys during the winter months or the animals were hibernating. The forest was more full of wild game in the lower altitudes, especially during the winter months. Also, this was the home turf of the vampires. Even the bears tended to fear them. The bears were smarter than me. I just hated the vampires.

I cursed internally as I struggled along the bear trail with low hanging tree branches and shrubs. I constantly had to press through the recalcitrant branches that kept grabbing and smacking me.

However, with each step I took back to the village I felt my blood madness subside. In my mind, I kept seeing the hurt in Abigail's eyes. It began to hurt me with a different pain of regret rather than rage. The realization of my cruel words and the hurt look in her eyes that had shone when I pierced her heart. Now the pain I had inflicted on her pierced my own heart. I closed my eyes tightly as if trying to physically squeeze out the image of her pleading eyes and produced single diamond-like tears that stayed in my eyes and didn't streak my face. I blinked rapidly in the darkened night for a few moments.

I could still hear David's psychic command in my head, "Kill! Kill! Kill!" But it was lessening.

A voice deep inside of me pleaded with me to go back to the Caverns of the Vampires and apologize to Abigail, but that was out of the question. Going back to the Cavern of the Vampires was suicidal. There were hundreds of vampires up there and they were out for my blood and revenge. I felt like that voice was truly me, but it was so buried by the overpowering madness that it barely registered and I only write this in retrospect.

That voice was a tether to sanity, but it hurt and added to the madness, so I pushed any anger or regrets aside, and for the rest of the hike, I kept my mind focused on the trail ahead and behind. I constantly kept wary of ambushes from any angle. I didn't nervously cast looks around but rather kept my peripheral vision open as Bryan and Critter had taught me. I did find that using peripheral vision put me in a simultaneous relaxed and alert state. If someone was alert with wide vision, their mind could relax because their body felt safe. If someone relaxed too much and lost their peripheral vision by staring blissfully into nothingness like a wannabe yogi, they would get scared at the benign drop of a pine cone. If they were alert with tunnel vision, the mind was aware that a lot of stuff was out of the immediate senses, so the mind worried and the movements became jerky with tension from the walk to the shifty eyes.

I chuckled insanely. I knew I was mad, if I hated everyone, including harmless yogis, but as much as I hated it, the insanity made me feel powerful.

I lost my thoughts and worries. My vigilance of the trail became a walking meditation. As the sun peeked over a distant ridgeline, the hike acted like an anesthetic. It mercifully numbed both my natural passionate attraction to Abigail's female form and my hatred for what she truly was beneath the skin. There was something else it numbed and that was my ambiguity. I knew that in her vampiric heart that she was indeed a good person, but I couldn't dwell on that. It brought back the stabbing pain of regret. A regret that I feared would kill me because of its lancing pain through my heart and mind..

With the numbness toward her brought by the safety of daylight, I found my fire growing against my own kind. The Mountain Warriors became the focus of my blood madness

"Kill! Kill! Kill!" I could still hear David's chant from beyond the grave embedded in my psyche. His disturbing mantra seemed to be building to a crescendo with each step down the mountain.

It had only taken a few hours to get to the Caverns of the vampires under Critter's lead. However he knew every shortcut. I only knew the general way back and that was to mostly just head down hill. After walking all night I would enter the camp at daylight in the early morning. I feared that I would never be sane again. I quickened my stride.

***

Tommy Laurens watched the videos of Eric walking back from the Caverns of the vampires. A drone hovered above him and Eric paid it no heed. Eric Hildebrande was a different man than the friend he had sent into the ravages of the Forbidden Zone not quite two weeks ago.

Eric had the same facial features and bodily structure, although a lot more muscular and in athletic shape, but there was something that almost made Eric unrecognizable to his friend.

Beneath the vampiric blood covering his face, the hard determination in his eyes appeared as if they were transplanted from the face of an ancient warlord. The sense of confident purpose in his stride was one that Gengis Khan would take when strolling through a smoldering, conquered, and pacified city, but anger simmered on his features. Even without the blood covering his face, Tommy was sure that Eric's skin would still burn red with underlying rage that blazed in his eyes. Whatever it was, if Tommy had not witnessed the transformation in the last two weeks through the videos from the drones, he probably would not recognise Eric right now. He was no longer the journalist, the spoiled and pampered adopted son of the Governor Hildebrande.

With Eric's interviewing skills and fearlessly jumping into combat to protect his new tribe, Eric, the former mild mannered reporter, had delivered a hit TV show. Tommy only regretted that, exiled and locked in the quarantined Forbidden Zone, Eric would never get to enjoy the rewards that he had earned.

Despite all that, Eric lived in an even more precarious position. He had pissed off a lot of people in high places. He was originally supposed to be making a documentary in the relatively safe and self-sufficient town of Craigsville, with a very capable security force. The story should have been a combination between a quaint Foxfire take of Appalachian folks surviving the brutality of the zombie/vampiric apocalypse. Instead, Eric was living in the heart of the terrors with the Mountain Warriors' tribe, and he had killed some very evil people and monsters who had been under the protection of the secret government. It was only his Uncle and adopted father, Governor Daniel Hildebrande, that provided any protection as well as the fact that the show was a hit among the population. Even better, the revenue that the show generated was raking in tons of money for the state, but Eric was constantly in danger from all sides.

As Tommy watched a wall of monitor screens, he heard a beeping alert from his official work cell phone. He stood up from his comfortable leather office chair and walked across the plush carpet. It was probably nothing, but even with his rank, Tommy had to take these alerts seriously.

He looked at the phone's screen. He collapsed in a chair and swore as he read the first few sentences of the text. His usual arrogant posture fled, and he slouched almost in defeat. He seemed to sink into himself the more he read the two page report.

The missive stated almost nonchalantly that his boss, Eric's adopted father, Governor Daniel Hildebrande, the ultimate power in the safe mid Atlantic states and the quarantined Forbidden Zone of the Southeast FEMA region, had been deposed in a nearly bloodless coup d'etat.

Tommy took a moment after reading the report, before he forced himself to stand up and pushed the phone across the desk. He stepped away and covered his forehead with his palm and slowly lowered his hand so that he rubbed his burning eyelids with his thumb and forefinger and then pinched the bridge of his nose to the point of pain.

"Oh damn," Tommy muttered. He could feel the blood leave his face. He began to pace.

"Eric's screwed with his uncle gone," he said to himself as he tried to shake off the sense of denial. Tommy meditated on that for a moment. Governor Hildebrande had been elected through some questionable tricks at the polls and ubiquitous corruption, but that was usual these days. There had always been a veneer of legitimacy in politics, even in the worst of times in the initial plague of zombism. To outright depose the Governor and report it as a common occurrence just struck Tommy as beyond odd and nearing insanity.

The people of the Forbidden Zone could probably care less. It was a continual state of chaotic anarchy already, where 90% of the population had died in the last two years from starvation, zombie attacks and fighting with other survivors. Tommy wasn't sure how the population of the Safe Zone would respond, but what could they do about it? The people followed politics but mostly, they were more concerned about the day to day worries of how to feed their families. This was nearly impossible because most of the sections of the world that provided food and energy were cordoned off to stop the spread of the plague. If the overthrow didn't affect their day to day life, they would probably shrug it off. What else could they do against the power?

The change might benefit some people. An entrepreneur could really make some money if he could exploit the quarantined land. Tommy of course had considered that, but the penalty of sneaking in or out of the razored wire boundary was an immediate bullet in the head and incineration. A trial for such a violation was a relic of better times.

Tommy collapsed into a chair again. Not only was his job, his friend's life, and not to mention his hit TV show in danger, but the already fragile stability of his country as well.

He saw another message appear. He read. It was from The Specter. He reread the message three times before it sank into his head.

Abigail was to be put to death. Today. In Craigsville.

Tommy dropped his phone from a suddenly nerveless hand.

| 2 |

Douglas cringed as he awaited impact from the hot lead as the man in the black fatigues quickly fired off ten rounds from the M-16 at almost point blank range. In shock Douglas realized that not one round hit him. That did happen sometimes when the stress of combat interfered with aim even in close proximity.

Despite the blood loss from his wounded leg and the energy expended from the last thirty yard dash up an almost sheer slope, as well as the adrenaline dump, Douglas gathered his remaining strength to attack the black clothed gunner and hopefully win an M-16. It seemed hopeless but he had to do something immediately.

He steeled his legs for a springing attack and looked up, but was surprised when he saw that the man in black was sighting the M-16 down into the valley rather than at him.

Douglas' mouth dropped. This man had to be a friendly person, but that seemed to be an impossibility way out here, far from his town. He studied the friendly gunner's grim face. It was bearded but vaguely familiar. The last time he saw this man he was a clean shaven.

Douglas said, "Josh? I mean, Captain Righter?"

"Josh is fine," his former boss answered in his relaxed drawl as he still scanned the valley beneath them. Josh had a calm, steady manner whether drinking a beer or shooting at a charging horde of zombies. Maybe his jawline tightened only slightly when shooting.

Douglas noticed that Josh's slitted eyes studied the scene below.

Douglas asked in amazement, "What are you doing here?"

"I am a fugitive from Craigsville, The Specter and the damn vampires like you." Josh said as he placed his cheek, almost as if affectionately cuddling the black plastic stock like a lover and easily squeezed off two more shots. A scream of shock and pain reverberated from below them as if shouting an answer to the rifle's report.

Josh brought his rifle down, and squatted behind the cover of the natural rock fortress with Douglas.

He gave Douglas his full attention. "I nailed two of them pretty good in the chest and winged a third, but we should go. Can you travel? How bad is your wound."

"I can hang with you. It's just a scratch, sir," Douglas said, putting on a brave face.

"Don't call me sir, again. Got that, brother? We're in the same boat," Josh said and sighted down the hill.

Josh fired a few more rounds as the darkness settled. Then all was silent and they waited.

Once night had fully settled, Josh said with his eyes focused on the darkness below them, "Stay here, Douglass. I'll be right back."

It oddly felt good to hear someone say his name after a week of running through the wilds alone.

Before Douglas could ask anything, Josh had disappeared into the gloom of the nighttime Appalachian forest. Douglas waited for a brief while and heard the report of Josh's rifle as well as a scream. Another minute passed and Josh reappeared with a second rifle slung across his broad shoulder. Josh unslung it and handed it to Douglas.

The former captain of the guard said, "It's a scoped 30-06. Unfortunately the dead guy wasted a few bullets after you. I only found eleven rounds for it. I did get two full magazines for my M-16, but you destroyed another guy's M-16 with a well placed shot."

"A lucky shot," Douglas corrected.

"Napoleon valued luck almost as much as cunning. There is an instinct to choosing the right place and time in a tense moment. Luck is just good split second decisions." Josh peered into the darkness with narrowed eyes. He then instructed, "If it comes down to it, let me do the bulk of the firing. Only shoot if you got a clear shot, but I prefer that we just retreat silently. It seems they are retreating to lick their wounds."

"You got it, Captain– I mean, Josh," Douglas stammered.

"Can you walk with that wound?" Josh asked.

Douglas nodded as Josh reached down and helped him to his feet. "I can run, if need be."

"We'll be moving swiftly but with as much silence as possible. Let's go," Josh ordered as if he was still Captain Righter of Craigsville's security force.

They marched for just over a half hour in the night and made it to Josh's shelter. It was located on a small flat spot up a steep hill with a cliff, towering above it. Douglas was happy at how well it was concealed. It was also in an inconvenient place where no one would just stumble upon them.

The front half was a lean-to made of branches and leaves and camouflaged well with the forest. A two feet thick blanket of loose leaves covered it making the roof look like the forest floor. Inside, Josh had a small fire pit with a covered, medium sized pot over the dead coals. Douglas could smell the scent of the remaining stew in the pot.

After spending a week in the woods with very little food and what he did have was unseasoned, Douglas could feel his mouth salivating as he could scent not just the squirrel meat, but the seasoning as well in the broth, particularly the wild garlic. He instinctively could tell it was flavored with salt. The scarce amount of food that he had over the last week had been without that vital mineral at all. His mouth immediately filled with saliva. There was also pepper and a few other spices he couldn't name off hand.

The back part of the crude shelter had a tarp covering Josh's sleeping area. Although extremely rustic, the sleeping area was well insulated with leaves, looked waterproof, and after sleeping under the clouds and stars, it looked very homely to Douglas. However, he was not sure how long his former boss would let him stay here.

Douglas stood stooped over under the four foot high roof.

"Have a seat and make yourself at home," Josh said. "Don't be so formal. You're my guest."

Douglas had a seat, awkwardly stretching out his wounded leg as he lowered his bottom gingerly to the ground.

"Oh hell," Josh said as he helped Douglas the last few inches down. "I forgot about the wound. I thought you were just nervous because I was your boss when I was in charge of law enforcement at Craigsville," Josh said "Craigsville" with the distaste as if a stink bug had flown in his mouth and he was spitting it out. "Let me get a fire going and I'll dress the wound."

With a cigarette lighter, Josh lit some birch bark under some small twigs and placed the new flame in a Dakota fire pit. The hole was dug a foot and a half into the rocky soil with a small connector tunnel to give it oxygen. The depth of the pit as well as the cover of the lean-to made the smoke and fire virtually invisible to anyone nearby. Even so Josh avoided using very dry wood, preferring slightly damp fuel and used a smaller amount of fuel to keep a dim, smoky fire. That way it wouldn't be so bright in the dark woods. In the daytime, Douglas knew that Josh would use the drier wood for a brighter, smokeless fire to keep his hiding spot hidden. It was a well known trick among those in the outdoors and survival communities, especially those hiding and on the run.

Douglas watched the fire hypnotically as Josh added more wood. The fire blazed strong and cozy, deep in the pit and a pot of water was placed on top. Josh added rags to the water in the pot to be sterilized in the boiling water. Then the former commander turned to Douglas. "Let's look at that wound.

Despite the pain and stiffness, Douglas quickly took his pants off. As a veteran from the war on terror, Douglas had seen that look in the eyes of the medics or soldiers acting as medics with the determination to cut the pants to get to a wound on the thigh. In the winter with just one pair of pants to his name, Douglas valued his britches as much as he valued a bullet for his empty handgun in his appendix holster even if the pants were already ventilated with a bullet hole.

"Tell me how you pissed them off," Josh requested as he studied the wound and began to clean it.

Douglas told the story of his most recent escape. When he finished he saw Josh looking with dismay at the wound.

"Is the wound that bad?" Douglas asked as he stared at Josh's worried face.

Josh shook his head, "Oh no. You'll recover fine. I was just thinking..."

"About what?"

Josh hesitantly said, "Hell, I don't know how to put this, but I owe you an apology."

"About what?" Douglas repeated.

Josh looked down and sighed. Douglas could see a mental load weighing on his old boss' usually calm face. Josh looked up towards the sticks and black plastic ceiling of the crude structure. "I suspected-- No, I knew that Craig was letting The Specter lead you to your deaths in that vampire cave. You and the three other soldiers. I knew it, but I didn't want to admit it."

Douglas shot a hateful glare at his caregiver.

"I deserve that look, but you knew as well as I did that we were feeding those damnable creatures with the town's petty criminals. The day after you left with The Specter, I was plotting Craig's overthrow. He is a puppet to The Specter, you know. I believe he's addicted to some designer drug. He is no better than a zombie. I wish I could help him. Deep inside, Craig is a good man, but not now."

"What happened there? You were Craig's number one go to guy," Douglas asked. The flash of hatred toward Josh had flamed and disappeared as fast as a firecracker's short glory.

Josh shook his head. "My status meant nothing. There's no hierarchy under a puppet controlled by a monster. I told my story to a damned journalist, believe it or not. I'm usually not stupid enough to talk to an agent of the press, but he seemed sincere, even if he was the Governor's nephew."

"The Governor's nephew?" Douglas whistled.

"Yeah. Eric Hildebrande. I'll kill that bastard if I ever get the chance. He was the last person I talked to. It had to be him who reported me."

"He sounds like an ass. How'd you escape?" Douglas asked.

"I was to be fed to the vamps as punishment, but I also had the loyalty of the men who took me there. I fought to escape, but I knew they let me go. The fight was more for show. They needed bruised and bloodied faces to have a convincing story. I delivered. I hope my men understood that. We didn't have time to chat, of course."

"Damned right they understand, sir," Douglas agreed. "You were always firm but fair. We'd follow you anywhere. To storm the gates of hell if need be!"

"Anyway, I may be headed back through those very gates of hell," Josh said with a faint hint of embarrassment at the exclamation of loyalty from Douglas, "But when I was to be fed to the vamps, the men were a bit lax as they were leaving me. I was able to escape my bonds, steal some guns and run off into the woods before the vampires arrived. I think Critter and Bryan battled them in my place. I heard a hell of a fight from way down the mountain," Josh paused and asked, "How in the hell did you escape? The Specter took you to their very lair, didn't he? I just went to their killing fields far from their caves."

Douglas told his story and ended with, "and I would have stood there stupidly hypnotized and let them butcher me had it not been for that vampiress. I was under some kind of mind control. She somehow broke us out of it and gave me this handgun."

Josh interjected, "One of the younger vampires helped you, I presume. I mean that female one who I think that you were talking about. Not too bad to look at either. She's pretty, whether a freak of nature or not, I mean."

Douglas nodded. "Her name is Abigail."

Josh looked at him and said, "You may not believe this, man, but she once talked to me in my head. Telepathically, I think. It was weird. Her mouth never moved, but I heard her clear as day."

Douglas nodded, "That's how she got me to run. That hideous thing they called The Mind, he had some psychic control over us. She broke that spell somehow."

"Yeah. There is some weird stuff going on. They say that psychic stuff is science, tapping into the electromagnetic impulses of the neurons, but I think it's demonic, and I plan to end it," Josh stated in an even determined tone, no trace of bravado. "I'm sure I still got support in Craigsville. I can stir things up and throw The Specter and the vamps out once and for all. Are you willing to go back to Craigsville with me?" Josh made a face like he bit into a lemon and added, "I hate that name, 'Craigsville.'"

Douglas looked excited for a moment but then shook his head, "No." He then said, "I'd love to, but I promised Abigail that I wouldn't go back to Craigsville. She didn't want me getting tortured and ratting on her."

Josh opened his mouth as if he would respond reasonably, but made a pinched face and swore angrily. "First off, who do you owe your loyalty to, the people of your town who you grew up with, who are being fed to these creatures or a vampiress who has access to your mind and may have altered you? Think man! If she can alter your thoughts to escape, she can alter your mind, period. Is your loyalty to her from your own virtue or from her diabolical power?"

Douglas thought about it, "She did what she thought was right. She chased me to an area where I was safe, gave me food, and a weapon."

"Coward! She bought your silence. I don't use the term 'diabolical' lightly. That mind stuff is evil. Demonic possession. No debate," Josh said. "You need to get your head out of your ass."

"Listen!" Douglas said firmly. "I can be reasoned with, but don't shout at me or call me names. As you stated, you're not my boss anymore!"

"You are right, man. I'm sorry. I have been stuck here for over a week rethinking every mistake that I made. Every evil that I pretended not to see. Pretending I wasn't sending good men to their death out of fear for my own skin, in disbelief that this was happening. I've been making every plan imaginable. I swore my life to the defense of liberty and justice when I joined the Army years ago to fight for this country's freedom. Although I left the Army, I still hold that oath to the constitution to heart. It tears me apart that I went along with feeding simple vagrants, petty thieves and probably innocent people on trumped up charges to the vamps. I had never witnessed what happened, but by God, I knew. I knew! I followed orders like a robot. A flunky for evil. All I can think about is how I could have ended it, or how I can end it now. Instead I sit here on my ass in this damn hovel!" Josh finished by slamming his fist against a supporting beam, almost collapsing the small structure on themselves.

Douglas stared at Josh. His former boss, one of the toughest men he ever knew, looked on the verge of crying. Not in weakness but emotional with impotent determination. He actually looked stronger with the eyes tearing up, not weaker. His face was stark granite, hard, but his eyes had the spark of jewels in the fire light. The man was passionate about freeing his people and would gladly give his life.

Douglas picked his words carefully at first and then slowly worked himself into a raging infernal of phrases. "I can follow you. However, we do not go in like lambs. If I go in with you, it's do or die. I am not getting captured, and I will keep my word and not rat out the vampiress, Abigail. We free Craigsville from Craig, The Specter, the vamps and that horrible name! Freaking Craigsville! What the hell? Either we change it or die in a hail of bullets. I am done living like an animal here in the wilderness, sir. From this point on, I live or die like a man! There is no gray area!"

Josh reached across the campfire saying, "Do or die. I can think of no one who I would rather have by my side, brother."

"My brother of another mother!" Douglas said with fire in his eyes as he sealed his words with a firm handshake. That was the only contract that they needed between them.

"Now let's get you bandaged up," Josh said as the water with the rags was boiling.

Douglas said, "Thanks. I'll be ready to walk back tomorrow."

"Not just me, but your family and friends back in town are counting on it."

**

It was night as Abigail watched Eric's back. Her night vision gave her a clear sight as if it was daylight. She didn't blame him, but rather pitied him. She had suffered the blood madness that comes when a vampire's gore contacts an uninfected human. Vampire blood felt like needles on the skin and a sword through the heart and mind, not to mention the psychic assaults. When she experienced it as a human before getting turned into a vampire, that madness had made her want to kill everyone until it was washed off of her skin. For nine months she battled the vampires alone, always on the run, always hiding, always fighting until they inevitably caught her.

Even more when she had offered her mind to Eric, it was to further bond them together, but it backfired horribly. Vampires would let their minds meld together with those who they care for. It usually calmed them and made them feel closer. She had never tried it before with anyone and it just happened naturally with Eric due to their mutual affection at the moment.

She loved Eric and she knew that he loved her. However in Eric's state, the mind meld was too much, and it caused the madness to increase more. If she had been thinking clearly she would not have entered his mind with him in that state, but after all they had been through together, the pain from her injuries and exhaustion of fighting at his side, she just naturally let her mind bond with him as vampires did, unconscious of what she was doing.

She wasn't taking control of him, they were giving control to each other. It was common for vampires to play mental tricks on each other. It was part of the courtship to test each other's mettle. Other vampires had tried it on her, like David.

Vampires were government experiments and they were told who to mate with for more powerful vampiric offspring. She resisted the duress to be with David, the mate that they chosen for her. It infuriated her and she fought bonding mentally because she hated him and the whole vampire program that she had been forced to join and would gladly be damned before producing a vampiric offspring with David.

With Eric, she instinctively went with it. She understood his reaction in his maddened state, but it hurt her none-the-less that he didn't trust her after all they had been through together.

But now she had nowhere to run. Her coven had established a mental connection with her that was as powerful as a homing beacon. She understood Eric's desire to kill all vampires, including herself, but it hurt her deeply in her beating heart that he said as much to her. The only person she loved turned against her even if it was the blood madness that caused it.

Night. It was her time to hunt animal prey for their blood. Instead she returned to the Caverns of the Vampires. It wasn't just her prison. It was the only place that accepted her nature, but the other vampires knew that she wasn't one of them in her heart. She also had to return to her cell to heal. Her injuries were almost fatal, even for a vampire. She had kept the severity of her injuries secret from Eric.

She headed inside the caves, back to her bed, and lay there unable to sleep. It was the night and despite her need for rest, she was nocturnal.

3

I could smell the oily scent of roasting bear meat. My mouth watered as I realized that I was within a mile of home. My stomach growled wretchedly, reminding me that it had been quite a long time since I last ate. I realized that I was nearing exhaustion and my mind was off. I actually had a pound of deer meat yesterday afternoon that was offered by the people under the protection of the Nunnehi, beneath the Caverns of the Vampires, but I felt a raging hunger that temporarily pushed that memory from my mind. Once again, I brushed aside the worry that I was losing my mind.

The trickle of a small stream caught my attention in the dismal valley. I stopped at the stream that cut through the deep wild and wooded valley. Despite the early morning it was still relatively dark, buried between two towering mountains. I attempted to wash the vampire blood off of my arms and face with the frigid winter water from a small creek. I had to crack the thin layer of ice over a small clear pool to access the water. I should have washed sooner.

Earlier, I attempted to clean myself, but it was a more ritualistic splashing of water on myself than a deep scrub, but as I neared the settlement, I became even more self conscious of the vampires' blood that still coated me. It would freak out the people of the tribe, to say the least, to show up after a few days in the Cavern of the vampires covered in blood, especially over my face.

However, no matter how much I tried to clean in the near freezing water, I could still see that nasty red, black dried blood everywhere. It clung to me under my black encrusted fingernails, sticky hair, and pores, I would have to boil my clothes and take a steaming hot bath to truly clean myself.

The worst article was my outer coat. I submerged in and wrung it out many times, but it was defiled with blood to the deepest thread. The under layers of my jacket, bodycam vest, and my shirt weren't too bad and I didn't want to wet all my clothes in the freezing weather, so my undergarments stayed dirty and I tossed the wet coat over my shoulder.

My pants looked like I waded through a fresh charnel house, but I couldn't take them off and do anything about that in this weather.

I made my final approach to the village on full alert. I was within fifty meters when I spotted the guard. I was tempted to sneak up on him. He was standing, leaning against a tree, half asleep. It was a kid, about fifteen. I didn't know his name, nor, at this moment, did I care.

I casually walked up and lightly slapped him across the face. He jumped awake fearful that I was Bryan and would kick his ass or subject him to a brutal punishment for his inattention. However when he saw me, he startled even more as if he was seeing a ghost. It told me that I had been written off as dead.

I furiously pushed him aside as he attempted to stop me. The look on his face told me that the word from my "friends" in the tribe was that I was permanently gone. They left me for the merciless undead while I still had my full fight with me. A core rule of the Forbidden Zone was to never leave a man behind to the savagery of the zombies or vampires. Inside, I raged that to save their own necks, they were willing to sacrifice me to the vampires, something worse than death in my opinion.

With eyes blazing for revenge, still under the blood madness of the slain vampires and chants to "Kill! Kill! Kill!" from David, I marched past the young guard into the village of the threadbare tarps. I drew my sword but let it hang nonthreateningly at my side. I was in no mood to be harassed for my return. The kid stayed away from me, but trailed behind announcing my return with worried shouts.

Adam was the first to see me as the sleepy guard realized his folly. The guard needlessly yelled, "An intruder approaches!"

An intruder was anyone who was a complete outsider, or it could be a long-time resident who may have been bitten and infected by a zombie or a vampire. Because of this knowledge, the insult of the label intruder compounded my madness. I felt the same unthinking rage return that I had when I cursed Abigail. She hadn't deserved it, but these damn betrayers did, I reasoned in my insanity. Rewetting the vampire blood on my face only reintroduced me to the needling pain rather than calming it.

Adam was startled for the briefest of moments. It was more of a flash of fear that I saw in his eyes behind his glasses, but he calmed and replied in his dry, Zen-like wisdom, "As we can already see, sleepy head, Eric has returned." He said to the guard. Then he replied to me, "Eric, it is good to see you."

Adam started to speak to me more, but I walked past him as if he didn't exist. I glared at three people who didn't hunt or fight, but worked around the camp. I had yet to make up my mind whether they were legitimately unable to do the more death defying chores due to disability or if they were simply slackers. Regardless, I gruffly ordered them, "Draw me a hot bath, and boil some water to disinfect my clothes." When they hesitated, I snapped, "Now!"

Still covered in blood and angry in disposition, I inspired a spastic rush in them as they followed my direction. In retrospect, I'm sure that my eyes glowed psychotically. I paid them no further attention, and I walked to my hootch.

When I was within twenty paces of where it should have been, I realized that it had been torn down. A rage that felt compelled from an outside force smoldered, like a powder keg's fuse smokes before detonation. David's long dead voice echoed in my mind, "Kill! Kill! Kill!" and the chant was turning into a scream again.

Despite feeling like the power of spilled vampiric blood controlling my anger came from beyond, I felt justified in my rage and reveled in its feeling of raw, unholy power. However, I wanted my explosion to have an effect on someone, an object of my fury, not mere workers.

Adam called at my backside, "You are breaking protocol coming this deep within the village without the proper inspection for bites."

I didn't even look at the chief.

"Shut up!" I commanded him in a harsh bark-like voice.

I was aware of the sudden cessation of all conversation throughout the camp. I was the center of attention. No one treated Adam with disrespect even in disagreement. It wasn't just the words, but I said it in a scolding tone that I would address a dog barking at its shadow who woke me from a deep sleep.

He paused for a moment as he attempted to recapture his bearing. Adam said a little more sternly but well in control of his anger, "Protocol must be maintained."

I could hear his boots rushing to catch up to my long strides. In his seventies, the man moved more pantherlike than most men half his age.

This protocol that he demanded was for those suspected of being bitten. It involved stripping completely naked in a tent and getting looked over for any bite or laceration that could result in a zombie or vampire infection. Everyone in the Forbidden Zone had a story of somebody who appeared healthy but turned into a zombie and attacked when least expected.

Part of the original protocol of this ville stated that people could not leave the village alone. There had to be at least two people leaving together on such an adventure. Ever since our encounter with the power of the vampires' psionic abilities, we were no longer allowed to travel with less than three people in a group. Four was the preferred number. Only Bryan and Critter were allowed to leave and return alone as they wished because of their uncanny woodsman and fighting skills, but even they didn't do that as often these days.

"You can gawk and check me out as I take a bath," I said with disgust, as if he were simply a peeping pervert. "Meanwhile, I want my hootch restored," I commanded as if I expected him to personally do it himself, as if he was my personal servant.

Adam stood speechless. The sound of his boot steps following me ceased momentarily. It gave me a perverse feeling of triumph. I had verbally slapped him to the point that his koans and pseudo-wisdom were rendered pointless. Usually, that was what had endeared me to him. Now it infuriated me. Everything infuriated me. Even the sound of my own breathing.

I also realized that the reason for his shock was the challenge to his authority. For a moment I again remembered Abigail's warning of blood madness from contact with vampiric blood. I felt the sudden urge to be rid of the filth on me realizing that

that was indeed the cause of my anger and my insubordination. I needed a cleansing bath more than anything.

"Halt right now, Hildebrande, or you will be struck down where you stand!" Adam commanded in a booming scream, deep and solid enough to almost shake the mountains around us.

"Try it, asshole!" I said, barely casting him a side glance.

That sealed my fate. It wasn't that I disregarded Adam's commands. It was my disregard of the rules. Adam was just as subject to them as anyone else.

"Hurry with my bath!" I ordered the camp workers as I ignored his building rage.

They already had a large cauldron heated for the daily chore of washing clothes. They looked confused as if not knowing whose words to follow, my orders shouted with insane eyes, blood on my face, and a blood encrusted sword in my hands or the standard protocol. The protocols were what they should have obeyed, but in my near psychotic condition, they were unsure.

The stickiness of the drying vampire blood was driving me nuts as I felt covered with stinging disease. The blood also felt like I had thousands of needles piercing my skin. It felt as if the washing that I had performed in the frozen creek only spread the pestilence excruciatingly deeper into my pores.

"Move! Now!" I bellowed.

They scrambled to take the large cauldron over to the tent with the bathtub.

I started to follow, but Adam seemed to suddenly appear before me. I stopped. His sword was drawn but not at the ready. It simply hung in his grasp at his side like mine. He presented no physical impediment for the moment. However the tone of his voice told me that would soon change.

He said calmly yet firmly, "Eric, place your sword and rifle on the ground and submit, now."

"Come and take it," I said, quoting the Spartan King Leonidas. I brought the point of my sword up from the ground so that it pointed at Adam's face and stared at him with a clenched jaw and slitted eyes.

"If that is your wish, very well," he said. He brought up his sword so that it was now pointed at my abdomen. If I proceeded on with my destination to the bath, I would impale myself. Then he lowered it to point at the ground as if wishing a peaceful resolution, but I knew that to be a facade.

"There is no need for this," he said diplomatically.

"You are right. I told you that I would submit once my bath--"

I did not have time to finish. He stepped forward as if to pat my shoulder with his left hand to calm my demons. I didn't relax. Everything was not as it seems. Everything could be a feint, including a friendly gesture. Adam himself had instructed me in the past. Seemingly out of nowhere, his blade flashed toward my head driven by his right hand and guided with his left, but instinctively the blade of my sword dropped to protect my abdomen as I stepped back and to the side.

My instinct proved correct. I had ignored his feint and blocked his true attack to my side. Our eyes glared into each other as our blades pressed. We both knew that that was to be a death blow. He smiled and relaxed. I let my shoulders drop knowing that he would swing when he saw me let go of the tension.

Again he feinted for my head but I blocked his real attack at my knee. He cursed. I could see genuine frustration growing in his eyes. He swung at me again and I realized that it wasn't just the training I had with padded swords in DC nor the training that Bryan, Critter and even Adam had taught, but rather, I was reading Adam. I wasn't sure if it was from Abigail's psionics, or just a combination of that and training. Maybe it was the mental influence of the vampire's blood that empowered me. However, I couldn't read his thoughts as written sentences. I didn't feel anything mystical, rather, I just knew. I just knew.

His movements, facial expressions, and maybe even his very thoughts betrayed his every intent. I could see things with clarity that I never would have noticed before I entered the Forbidden Zone nor even the day before now. At first every one of his initial moves was a fake or a series of fakes before an actual attack. In the past I would have been fooled and flinched at every fake. Not now.

After swinging and getting blocked at every effort, Adam's frustration mounted. Savagery overtook him. Soon, he no longer faked but furiously attacked as his anger took hold. His speed and power would put a man half his age to shame.

His fury increased as my mocking smile grew. Eventually, he had lost all of his control and came at me with full rage and violence totally absent of skill, but full of power from years of training. Yet always, my sword stayed between me and his furious slashing steel like a moving wall. Either that or I moved to the side or ducked at the right time, always a step ahead of his vicious onslaught.

I felt my confidence growing and warned myself of cockiness. Adam was deadly as a rattler even at his worst, maybe more so.

I stepped back as I heard Shelley, the camp's herbalist and healer, scream from behind me, "Stop, you two."

Adam took advantage as I turned to look at her and he swung at my face. I ducked and slashed up at his head, and my sword crashed into his skull as his sword flew past me. Adam, the camp's elder, combat instructor, head chieftain, and wise man, collapsed in a heap at my feet.

I stepped back as Shelley ran to him. She went to her knees to protect him from me, but I accomplished all I desired. I just wanted a soaking bath.

She looked over his head for a gash wound from my blade. When she couldn't find a laceration or cleft in his the bony cranium, she looked up at me with confusion.

I told her with my anger at a controlled simmer, "I hit him with the back of the blade only to save you the grief. When he comes to his senses, tell him if he approaches me with violence again, I will not be the slightest bit merciful. Everyone of his strikes at me was meant to kill or permanently disable. I will not let that happen again without equal force."

"But protocol," she said. "You needed to be checked."

"I agreed to it. You can check me as I bathe," I said to her and then turned my anger to all the camp who stood around me. I had the attention of all fifty tribal members who had gathered around to view the spectacle. I continued, "but I will not be treated with the disrespect you show me. All of you! I am not some idiot to be treated like a dog. If I am left for dead by you in the Caverns of the Vampires, and return uninfected, I demand the same treatment that Critter and Bryan get. I have proven that I can handle the dangers of the Forbidden Zone, better than anyone else in the camp."

They stared in shock, but no one disputed me at this moment. The fact that I stood against Adam, and still stood upright was almost as shocking as returning from the Caverns of the Vampires as an uninfected man.

I ignored them and walked to the hootch with the bathtub.

When I entered, I saw that the tub was full of steaming hot, clear water from a nearby spring. My aching joints seemed pulled like a magnet toward the warmth. A large pot of water simmered over a small fire next to the tub. The smoke disappeared into the hole at the top of the tarp tent. It was set up like a teepee. I knew that the smaller kettle was to disinfect my clothes. I stripped but before I threw my clothes in the pot, I wetted a clean towel in the hot water and wiped my body down. I wanted as much of that blood off of my skin as possible so it would not surround me in the bathwater that

I would soak. I really needed a hot shower, but that was out of the question in this wilderness camp.

When I was satisfied that I washed most of it off my naked body, I tossed the soiled towel into the caldron with my clothes and then stepped into the tub. The shock of hot water was painful but I felt the heat seep into the marrow of my frozen bones. I didn't realize how cold I was from the hike back in the frigid, wet weather that had plummeted below freezing. A numbness to pain can really accentuate the pleasure when warmed. I was in heaven as I slowly succumbed to the luxury of the hot bath water up to my neck.

I slid into the water gingerly and sighed in ecstasy once I was submerged up to my chin. I then dunked my head beneath the surface and vigorously ran my fingers through my hair to clean it. I was pleased to see that the water was not too stained with a horrible red of the blood of my enemies. It felt good to have that burden off of my body.

As the simple pleasure of a hot bath ensconced me and the blood of vampires left me, my sanity slowly returned. The full weight of all of my actions slammed onto my shoulders. I had threatened Abigail. Although a vampire, she helped me and I deeply care for her. I left her to return to her brood when she was ready to leave with me.

Then, I nearly killed Adam. Deep inside I loved and respected him as a leader and a man of good character. Even if he would avoid me in the future, I knew I could never let my guard down around the old master. I also knew that the rest of the village would probably be demanding my blood for the infraction as well as ignoring the protocols that he had been representing. Granted the talk about me would be behind my back as I could see on their faces that they did not have the balls to confront me at the moment.

My worries turned to fear as Bryan, the camp's warchief, limped into the tent on a homemade crutch from a gnarled branch. I had forgotten his grave wound to the leg in the Cavern of the Vampires. I kept my face calm as I spoke in a friendly voice, en garde for deception, but I sat up from my near reclining position in preparation for a possible attack from the camp's second in command. My sword and firearms were within easy reach. He watched me as I glanced at my weapons, but he showed no inclination to fight.

I really did fear the warchief. Not just because my sanity had returned and I understood the consequences for my actions, but because he had regularly humiliated me when he trained me in the past. I had been at their mercy for two weeks and they never missed an opportunity to rub my face in it, but no more.

"How's the leg?" I asked, wanting to keep the conversation off of me for the moment.

"It's been better. I'll probably be laid up in camp over the next week. I guess that's a good thing since I will have to assume temporary command ever since you knocked out our leader, Adam."

The casualness in the tone surprised me.

"How is he?" I asked with genuine concern now that the madness had worn off.

"He's still unconscious," Bryan said as he looked me straight in the eyes.

My eyes darted sideways to my sword and rifle.

He shook his head and said, "Don't sweat it. We shouldn't have left you behind the vampires' caves. They abandoned me too. I was in there for over a day with Scott and Critter."

I blinked in surprise. I thought that they had all run out together.

Bryan continued, "If I wasn't laid up, I would have handled things differently when you returned."

I was about to ask Bryan how he was abandoned in the cave, and more importantly how he made it back, but I was deeply surprised and silent. At that moment, Bryan's son, Bradley, darted inside the tent. His father turned and scolded him, "How many times have I told you to knock before entering a hooch."

"Uh, a lot," said the boy.

Bryan caught me staring at his son. I wasn't sure if he could read my surprise. In my desire for vampire blood, I had completely forgotten that the main reason for going there was to rescue the child from the vamps after The Specter had kidnapped him. All I could think about was killing David. That had been due to Abigail's psychic influence to prod me to leave rather than slow down her rescue, I deduced.

But I wondered how exactly the boy got out of the caves.

Bryan said, "I got to thank Abigail when she gave him back, but I wanted to thank you personally as well for having rescued my son. I mean it. He means more to me than my own life."

The feeling in Bryan's eyes was something I had never seen in his usually hard visage before and I realized that his believing that I helped rescue his son was probably the only reason why he didn't kill me for my disrespectful insubordination to Adam.

I nodded, still stupefied. I hated taking credit for the rescue that Abigail had accomplished solely on her own. I also hated my dishonesty in my silence, but for my survival, I determined that now was not the time to confess.

After receiving his father's rebuke for entering without knocking, Bradley ran up and hugged my neck with such zeal that he seemed oblivious that he got my bath water all over him. "Thanks so much. I love you and Abigail!"

"Go play, Bradley," Bryan said as he smiled warmly at his son. Bradley happily left the tent.

Bryan looked back at me and continued, "Although I understand you were under duress when you gave him over to the vampiress, and I am sure you know her better than us to trust her, but I must admit that I was surprised when it was a lone vampire who returned him even if it was Abigail. I owe both you and Abigail my life. You probably won't get the total freedom to come and go like Critter and me, but we will treat you as a full member from now on."

When I sighed in relief, his suddenly stern voice chilled my now warmed marrow, "but you must follow protocol from now on. There is no exception for anyone! And you need to apologize to Adam when he wakes up."

Again I nodded dumbly, but I wanted to say that I would never have handed a human child over to a vampire, no matter how friendly or attractive she may seem, but I wasn't sure if that would incriminate me.

"Abigail looked pretty beat up," he said as he continued to look at me.

I nodded and explained, "Abigail and I killed The Mind. He crushed her chest when he grabbed her. I heard her ribs snap. If she was human, she would have died instantly. Even so, I still thought that she was in mortal danger."

It was odd to see Bryan's eyes widen with surprise. He was usually one of the most stoic people I had ever met, other than Critter, of course. "Is she still in danger?" Bryan asked. "Surely The Specter and the other vamps know of her assistance to our cause. I am sure that David--"

"I killed David. His head is smashed beyond repair and about a mile from his body. I think he will stay that way, this time. Richard promised me that David will never rise again."

Again he showed his surprise. Bryan had beheaded the stout vampiric enforcer only to find him reassembled, very much alive, and out for revenge when we entered the caverns.

"Whoa," he said as he looked at me with even more respect. "So how did you escape, unbitten? Abigail?"

"Yes. She helped. Also, David attempted a coup d'etat against Richard. It failed and Richard, even though he had a gun at my back, let me take David's head and wished me well."

"So Richard is," Bryan hesitated before saying the word, "friendly?"

"I am not sure. I got the feeling that they are trapped under The Specter's rule. A force of the Specter's human soldiers entered the caves and threatened Richard. I sliced into the humans' throats so that the failed vampires would become blood crazed and attack the people as a diversion so I could escape-- those soldiers were traitors to humanity anyway. Richard and David were terrified about how The Specter would respond. Trust me, I do not think the vampires were accidents. They are living experiments."

Bryan nodded in thought with distant sage eyes as he said, "Deep inside, I knew they weren't accidents but I preferred to not act as though I was certain to avoid more questions about the reality of our screwed up situation. We've got more than enough worries with just staying alive."

"Do you need to check me for bites?" I asked as I started to stand in the tub.

"No, I can see in your eyes that you are fine. As I said, you'll be treated with more respect and get more freedoms. In return, never attack Adam or anyone else again."

"I can't defend myself?" I demanded.

His face suddenly hardened like the granite cliffs above the camp, "We both know that you were out of order and provoked the attack. You know damned well you are free to defend yourself, just don't be a jackass about it."

I nodded and wondered if Bryan was in better health if we would be crossing swords. Adam, Critter, and Bryan were the main chiefs of the tribe. With Adam temporarily out due to me, Critter hunting and Bryan wounded, there was little they could do to me even if they desired. Also, Bryan did seem genuinely grateful for me slaying David and The Mind as well as rescuing his son.

"Enjoy the bath," Bryan said with a courteous nod. Then he limped out.

After he left, I blew out a breath of air. Since arriving they had hammered into my head to be aware of my breath, because holding the breath hindered thinking and more importantly, it locked up the muscles in combat just when you needed free and agile movement the most. I thought I had been breathing, but maybe not fully. I decided to ask at our next training session. That is if they would still train me when Adam came back to his senses.

I then took another deep breath, submerged my head beneath the warm water, and blew it out as I thought of Abigail. Now that I had the vampire blood off of me and my sanity returned, I fully regretted treating her the way that I had. I had been regretting it all along, but each moment that went by it bothered me more until it was a physically crushing ache in my heart and mind. I hoped she would understand. She had warned me of the madness. She told me that she had been afflicted with it herself when she was still human.

A deeper pang of guilt hit me-- Nine months of battling and then to be changed against her will... I swore out loud as it dawned on me that I may be the closest thing that she had as a friend and I rewarded her with a curse and a death threat.

I pushed any guilt from my mind. The vampires were an evil spawn and she was supposed to turn me. Although she feigned disobedience to The Specter, Richard and whoever was ultimately in charge of them, I couldn't help but wonder if that was all part of the plan to chip away at my willingness so that I would be turned as she was turned. I wondered about that in the paranoia that the Forbidden Zone and constant psychic attacks from vampires inspired, but I knew she was good and I was only trying to justify my horrible behavior.

I dunked my head under the blood-warm water. It was no longer hot and was slowly becoming an uncomfortable lukewarm. I splashed it over my head when I surfaced. I did this a few more times to really wash anything filthy away.

I firmly decided that if I was to maintain my humanity, I had to avoid Abigail at all cost. She had admitted to drinking human blood of people already killed by her coven and that human blood passed around in a large chalice. She actually killed her first human victim as the bloodlust was most powerful. From what I understand, the desire for blood is overpowering when a vampire is first turned. She tried to explain that the woman she killed was responsible for her getting caught by Richard's group and she was an enemy, but still, that didn't sit right with me. A truly good person would never kill another person for blood, no matter how deserving the person was of death. Abigail had also killed a crazy scientist named Dexter. She drank his blood only to make it look like he was killed by a horde of failed vampires. But human blood was as intoxicating as whiskey as well as revitalizing for vampires where animal blood only fed them. I couldn't help but wonder about her motives. Maybe I wondered that simply to placate the stabbing regret in my heart. No. I didn't wonder. I knew I was wrong. Nonetheless, I had to avoid her and all vampires.

I again submerged my head and felt an electric jolt in my head. I saw Abigail's face full of terror.

She and I had a psionic connection that I had tried to turn off when I threatened her earlier. It was also reduced after The Mind was killed and the Nunnehi cut off the Flow, as they called it, but somehow she had burst through my mind. However, I sensed that it wasn't intentional.

I tried to reconnect with her as I could sense great panic in her heart, but I realized something had cut the mental link between us. However, I couldn't deny that I sensed the intense horror that she felt. Before the link was cut off, I saw the masked, skeletal face of The Specter, leering into her eyes, and then mental blackness, like she was snuffed out of existence.

I tried to tell myself that it was her mind games, a trap, but I knew that it wasn't. We had settled that she was on the side of good. Everything that I felt before against her was to cope with the guilt of my atrocious action and words toward her.

The water cascaded off of my body as I unconsciously bolted to my feet in the tub. I found the hilt of my sword and instinctively and firmly gripped it in my hand. I set it down as I grabbed a towel and hurriedly dried off and dressed in the folded, cleaned clothes that those who drew my bath water had left.

I had work to do, but I wasn't sure what that work was, yet, but rather an intense desire to do something, anything.

| 4 |

The sunlight filtered in through the deep crystal walls of the Caverns of the Vampires. In a room devoid of any man made creation, Abigail would come to this location for solitude. A small spring gushed forth from the ceiling and trickled down the quartzite wall, formed a small pool the size of a bathroom sink, and disappeared into a hole in the cavern's floor. The bubbling sound of the water always calmed her soul.

She sat cross legged on the sandy floor and watched a stray beam from the sun trickle through the crystal above. She pulled the sleeve of her black vampiric uniform up her arm and moved the bare skin of her wrist so that the light touched her on the back of her arm. She turned and moved her arm to let the beam touch different parts of her before it burned. The light had passed through many meters of crystalline rock. She watched the small dim ray with longing as it shot to her pale skin. She experienced dread and a gnawing pain in her gut full of regret, knowing that she could never see the majestic beauty of a sunrise or sunset again.

The way she moved the beam of sunlight across her skin, she was reminded of an odd habit from her childhood. She had always loved the outdoors and desired to be close to nature, to fully live it. One thing she did as a little girl was to allow a wasp or a spider, especially black widows, to crawl on her hand. It would awe the other children in her group. She reveled in their praise of her bravery, but she knew that she was in no danger. As long as she showed no fear or aggression, the insect or arachnid would explore her hand as she rotated it to always give it a flat spot to walk. The difference was that the sunlight would actually hurt her whether she showed fear or not.

She again placed her hand under the beam wishing she could increase the time of her contact through discipline and acquire tolerance for the sunlight. Abigail did not relish being a creature of the night. She bit her lip for a few seconds and then yanked her hand away as her skin started to burn intensely hot. Direct sunlight could cause her skin to literally smolder. She could go out in the daylight only with the thick hooded cloak, dark sunglasses, and sunblock lotion. She spent moments like this trying to get her skin used to the light, but inside she knew it was pointless. She was eternally a person of darkness as long as she suffered the infection.

She placed her hand back under the beam and winced. The pain of the light temporarily hid the pain inside her. She thought of Eric. She thought of her lost humanity.

She had never wanted to be a vampire. She only agreed under the delirium of pain, fever, and a quickly approaching death. Without full consent, most new vampires went insane through the infection process as the mind expanded with psychic connections. It was far worse than the bloodmadness that came from the mere contact with vampiric blood. Most died of the insanity overload. The vast majority who survived as vampires, lived a psychotic life of madness inspired solely by bloodlust. Only a select few maintained their intelligence and excelled with the new powers. She was one of the few intelligent vampires who were actually more gifted after the transformation.

On the night that she was turned into a vampire, she almost succumbed and died of insanity. Some of it was pain, but even worse, she could hear the thoughts of every sentient being around her. The vampiric brain picks up every electromagnetic field put off by a neuron. The psionic powers were based on the science of physics not metaphysics or magic. The jumbled thoughts that were once hidden suddenly became heard all at once. She could hear the desires, heart break, dreams, yearnings and fears of everyone around her, even animals. Those fears became her own. She heard the thoughts of people near her and felt compassion for the humans, but she also wished to kill them by draining them of their blood. The internal conflict maddened her even more at the time. Somehow her mind handled it all despite the obstacles of her mental resistance. Somehow she survived and retained a shred of her humanity and that was the rarest. It was a small spark of humanity that had grown over the last year. Now she desired to be fully human again. However she was aware that such a transformation back was nearly impossible, and the one true friend she had, Eric, had sworn to kill her just last night. She understood the madness. She herself had felt it. It wasn't him saying and doing what he did, but it still hurt her worse than the fractured ribs.

Because of her resistance to the vampiric process, she never really bonded with any of the other vampires. Richard was the only one who she somewhat cared for and he was a very distant father figure, who she loved but constantly felt rebellion toward. She had more affinity toward humans who feared her and who drove her bloodlust. Eric was the only one whom she had felt at ease with. Not that she got to hang out with any other people the way things were.

Abigail thought of how she sat back to back with Eric, leaning on each other and talked about their goals, dreams, desires, and heartaches as they awaited their fate at the hands of the people under the protection of the mysterious Nunnehi. Later Abigail and Eric stood together looking over the precipice. At that moment she wanted to find a way to stay with him. Without turning him. She could sense that he felt the same. It was an impossible dream, yet they shared it, until she let her mind go. She knew she had unwittingly sucked in his psyche and let hers expand into his mind.

That was common for vampires, but for people especially someone suffering from the blood madness, that was too much. She brooded on that thought.

She wistfully smiled as she thought of Eric saying, "The brooding vampire. How cliche."

"Ouchy," she cursed, trying to keep her voice light in a vain attempt to affect her dour mood.

She yanked her arm away as she forgot about the weak sunlight on her hand. She rubbed the painful area in the webbing between her thumb and forefinger. It was the acupuncture point that was called Large Intestine Four. It was a balancing point for the body. She reasoned that sunlight on particular areas may heal her, but all the sun did was torture her as did her affinity for Eric.

A booming voice echoed through the caverns and shook her to her core. "Where is Abigail?"

It was the inhumanly low and gravelly voice of The Specter demanding her presence. He was in a far off passage, but voices echoed for almost an eternity in the caverns. It sounded like The Specter stood over her.

"I am not sure where she is, sir," she heard Richard reply in a whiny voice quaking with fear. Usually his tone arrogantly resonated with calm and an almost aristocratic nature, but he was audibly shaken.

She desired to go deeper into the caves where the people under the protection of the Nunnehi lived. She would probably face the death sentence that they warned her about on her last visit that was unwelcomed. Usually vampires were killed on sight. They withheld the death sentence from her because they sensed that she came in peace. She even scratched and massaged the gigantic feline that was supposed to immediately devour all vampires they encountered. Even the savage cat saw the goodness in her, but the people there warned her never to return unless invited. Such a future invite was highly doubtful.

She was tempted to ignore the threats of the people under the protection of the Nunnehi. Those people, regardless of their threats, were capable of mercy. The Specter wasn't. She was also sure a death at their hands would be quicker and more dignified than what The Specter had designed for her.

She froze as she heard the wet smack of a fist hitting flesh. Richard cried out in pain.

She took a deep breath in for courage and called to them, "I'm coming."

"Get your ass here, now!" The Specter boomed.

She stood up and did a light jog unsure of what to expect but dreading what was to come. Judging the way that the voice echoed to her, she guessed that he was a half mile away in the passages. Her chest stabbed as her breath increased in both volume and rate and tortured her fractured ribs.

Instinctively she wished to walk, not wanting to face The Specter, not wanting to show that his orders struck a sense of urgency in her, but she could not bear to hear Richard, her vampiric father, take anymore abuse.

"I'm coming," she repeated.

"Then move it!" The Specter barked like a Marine Corps drill instructor.

In a fearful, unconscious response to his command, she found herself sprinting. Her deep breaths punished her ribs even more that were still healing from the fractures last night. Vampires were resilient and recovered from fractures quickly, but she still needed another day or two.

Her black cloak billowed like a sail on a boat navigating the river Styx. Her black leather thigh high boots made whispering sounds on the sandy dirt of the cave's floor. A healthy young vampiress, she usually thrilled in the feeling of running, however her ribs started to sharply protest her deeper breaths even more. She slowed her pace slightly to steady her breath so as not to appear weakened before The Specter.

Abigail pushed onward down the cave at a light jog.

She turned a corner of the winding cavernous passage and found herself suddenly stopped as if she hit a cave wall. She felt like a vice clamped around her throat. She was lifted off of her feet and slammed into a crystal wall and was held by her throat with her feet dangling a head's height off the ground. She saw nothing but the flaring of The Specter's black cloak, his skull mask and his eyes full of fury. Not just the wrath of an angry man, but the fire that lit the eyes of a stone cold killer, enraged.

As she fought with the shock and lack of breath, she looked into the cruel dark eyes surrounded by the contrasting whites behind the skull faced mask. The Specter leaned in so that their foreheads touched, almost like lovers. The firm, iron grip beneath his black leather gloves slowly increased the pressure of the squeeze at her windpipe.

He yanked her towards him and then again slammed her into the wall. Her still healing shattered ribs screamed in protest, but it didn't reach her lips as all air was cut off from her lungs by his cruel hands on her throat.

He slammed her into the wall yet again and let her fall to the floor like a rumpled suit. She stared up at him and started to stand.

He planted a firm foot in her chest and slammed her against the wall again. She slid back down the wall into a painful heap.

"Stay on the ground, worm," The Specter bellowed.

She glared up at him as her anger flashed beyond her pain. She then glared at Richard who stood meekly behind the broad back and peeking over the broad shoulders of The Specter. The Specter and Richard were surrounded by Lucian, a young insecure vampire who at least had his wits and a few other of the intelligent vampires. There was also a mob of failed vampires, whose turning had so wracked and overwrought their minds that they were basically drooling idiots capable of only killing and following the simplest of commands if even that.

"Don't look at Richard, you are where you are because of your actions, not his," The Specter growled.

She stood up and ducked a thunderous blow from The Specter's fist. He glared at her as she stood her ground after he missed. She tasted blood that came up from her shattered chest wound. She swallowed it, not wanting The Specter to see her vulnerability. Standing her ground was all she could do. To further take on the Specter would result in instant death.

"What actions do I stand accused of?" she demanded.

"The Mind is dead. He was a work of scientific wonder. Bryan's kid is returned to the Mountain Warriors. My human soldiers are dead. David is dead," The Specter recited his litany of complaints against her.

She nodded and said, "It sounds like David got what he deserved for killing The Mind, your human soldiers, and freeing Bryan's son."

He tried to smack her face. As she ducked, his hand cuffed the top of her head and then he grabbed her hair. Abigail flashed her fangs at him. He slapped her across the face with a hand covered in a black leather glove and grabbed her throat again.

"You were to turn Eric Hildebrande into a vampire. You were underground with him for over a day and yet he walked away fully human. You cuddled like highschool kids over that cliff. Your mouth was inches from his neck, and yet!" The Specter said nothing more.

"Who made that slanderous accusation?" she coughed as he released her throat enough for her to choke out her demand.

He slammed his forehead into hers with almost concussive force, and she stared into his merciless eyes. A vision from a drone penetrated her mind. The Specter psychically imposed onto her a video of her and Eric in an embrace. Her lips were indeed inches from Eric's throat. She couldn't deny it. She didn't realize that The Specter had such psionic abilities.

"In your foolish passion for the human, you overlooked your mental jamming of the drone's footage. If you had turned him, he would have fully been your plaything by now."

Instinctively, she punched his shoulder and was rewarded with a howl from his lips as he let go. The knuckles of her fist felt the wetness of his blood from the shoulder wound from a bullet that he suffered the day before. Bryan's wife, Anna, had shot him when he had kidnapped their son.

He smacked her face again with the full weight of his body, slamming her against the wall. She painfully stayed on her feet and said, "That vision from the drone isn't proof of anything! It was your madman's dream."

A voice down the hall called to her. It sounded arrogant and dripping with oily slime, "Maybe not, Abigail, but my testimony is not a dream."

She looked as the speaker stepped into the hall. It was a short wiry vampire. She almost sank to the cave's floor in despair as she recognized him. She had never expected to see him alive again.

"Dexter," she gasped.

She had killed him a few days ago when he was a man or so she thought that he was dead. Some sick individual had revived him and now he stood before her as a fully changed vampire. He also no longer needed his glasses due to the regenerative properties of the vampiric virus.

"Yes. You killed me and left me for dead," Dexter said with a smile.

"Take her!" The Specter bellowed.

A few failed vampires grabbed her arms and Lucian stood with his hands hovering over her. He looked confused.

The Specter bellowed, "You don't need to ask her consent to check her for weapons, idiot!"

"Yes sir," Lucian squeaked.

She stood passively. Lucian quickly felt Abigail's body and disarmed her of any weapons he could find. The M-16 was unstrapped from her back, a 9mm Glock was taken from her hip, and her sword was removed from her waist as well as a combat knife and a multitool from her cargo pockets.

"What are you going to do with her?" asked Richard, the only thing close to a friend that Abigail had in this mad world.

The Specter glared at her with his arms akimbo as he stated, "She is going to Craigsville to answer for all the vampiric deaths that the town has suffered."

"She has only killed one person that I know of and that was under the madness of just becoming a vampire," Richard protested.

"Correct," agreed The Specter. "She obviously isn't one of us and should not be trusted. I would kill her now, but she would serve us better as a scapegoat."

The Specter turned his glare to Lucian and ordered, "Bind her arms and legs."

Lucian nodded to two failed vampires and relayed The Specter's order as he handed them a length of rope, "Do as he says."

They started to follow his orders, mumbling incoherently from their thick lips, drool dripped from their exposed fangs. They stared stupidly at the length of the parachute cord between them. An almost permanently confused look was welded to their faces as they tried to figure out how to perform the simple task of tying a knot around Abigail's wrists.

"No," barked The Specter as he cuffed Lucian on the back of the skull. "You do it yourself. I don't trust those idiots to tie a proper knot. She is not getting away this time."

The failed vampires stared stupidly as if unaware that The Specter insulted them.

"Yes, sir," Lucian said with more fearfulness than respect. However he bound Abigail's arms together with a relish. A cruel smile lit his face as he cinched the rope down on her wrists with a violent yank with both hands causing Abigail to gasp as the motion made its way up her limbs to her ribs.

Abigail glared at Lucian. She had killed his vampiric mate when she was still a human. He never forgave her and she could see he relished having her tied. Despite no love lost between the two of them, there was still the odd loyalty and bond between the high functioning vampires. There were only twenty of them who she knew of who hadn't succumbed to the madness of the failed vampires. However, there were thousands of the failed vampires that ranged from functioning idiots to complete drooling morons to psychotic imbeciles who lived only to kill anything in sight and drink blood. The last group were no better than zombies and usually were instantly dispatched, but The Specter was allowing these psychos to live as he built an army of them for an undisclosed reason.

When her wrists were bound, The Specter checked them himself and cinched the cords even tighter.

"Good job," he said to Lucian who looked proud of himself with the praise. The Specter then handed him another two lengths of green parachute cord and instructed, "Wrap this around her arms and body, and then wrap the other cord around her legs so she can walk, but not run."

"Where could I run?" Abigail demanded. "This is the only place I can call home."

Lucian tied the rope around her.

The Specter's skeletal mask grinned at her as he rumbled something that sounded like a growl. It was actually the closest that he usually came to a laugh.

The skull-faced man rumbled a reply, "Don't try the babe in the mountains routine on me. I know that you are very resilient, but we will find your limits today." The Specter said with a knowing look in his cruel eyes.

Despite the dire situation, she grimly smiled back at him. The Specter definitely called it right. Before the plague of the zombies and a year before they changed her into a vampire, she had lived alone in the Appalachian Wilderness surviving on primitive skills. Her goal was to write a book that she envisioned would make her a modern day, female version of Henry David Thoreau. That peaceful endeavor now seemed like several lifetimes ago.

The Specter jerked her shoulder and pushed her ahead with enough force to make her fall forward as her legs got caught in the rope restricting her gait, but he easily caught her before she hit the floor. She knew the catch wasn't due to kindness, but rather to show he had the power to make her final moments comfortable or miserable, but regardless, his end goal was to terminate her life very soon and very painfully.

As The Specter pushed Abigail toward the deeper bowels of the caverns Richard said, "It might be better to take a helicopter to Craigsville than the tunnels."

The Specter stopped and glared at him, "Why?"

"The Nunnehi shut off the Earth powers," Richard explained.

"Earth Powers?" The Specter scoffed. "That sounds like hippie crap. It's simply electromagnetic waves."

"Yes, sir," Richard replied, "Either way, they cut us off. Our psionics are down. It's not just the death of The Mind. We are cut off. The tunnels don't work."

"What about the tunnels?" asked The Specter with annoyed surprise as they continued to walk.

Richard motioned ahead at a large crystalline rock wall that blocked the passage where they were heading. It appeared to be a natural dead end. The rock face itself seemed to have been there since the dawn of time. They covered the distance quickly. At the wall, The Specter angrily pushed Abigail into it. She went with the push, bounced off the unyielding crystal wall and rolled to the floor.

The Specter then kicked and punched the wall that had not been there the day before.

The tunnels through these doorways compacted distance and even time as well in one occasion as witnessed by Eric. Craigsville was over thirty miles away, but through the tunnels of the Nunnehi, it was a thirty second walk. Now that passage was terminated.

After cursing, The Specter grabbed Abigail by the collar and lifted her up to his face. Although relatively tall at five feet eight inches, she was dwarfed by the masked giant. She looked up to him like a sparrow in the hands of a bully.

"This is your doing, vampiress!" The Specter yelled inches from her face.

"Are you intimidated that there are things bigger and more powerful than you?" she asked. Despite the dire situation, a smile found its way to her face as she saw the worry in his eyes.

He brought his fist back wanting to crash her face in right then but he instead growled in frustration. She knew that it wasn't mercy, but rather he had plans for her last day on Earth. He dropped her to the ground and radioed for a chopper.

| 5 |

I had stepped out of the tub, dried off, and quickly dressed in fresh clothes and loaded my weaponry on my body. I headed to my reconstructed tent and ignored the curious stares of the inhabitants of the village. I entered my dwelling and sat in solitude for a while.

Outside of my tent, I heard the clanging sound of pans, squeals and laughter of children, and the whispers of adults. The laughter of the kids was subdued. They had been trained not to be too loud to attract attention, but they were still kids, even in a zombie apocalypse. My paranoia imagined the whisper of adults to be much louder. I knew that I was most likely the subject of camp gossip.

Although I felt more like myself, I still felt a flickering flame deep in my heart that had been the burning anger from before. I realized that it was more than the superficial blood of the vampires on my skin, but rather something deep seated in me. Although I still heard the whispered chant of David to "kill," I was sick of being scared. Everywhere I had turned since arriving less than two weeks ago, I faced someone else who threatened me, tried to dominate me, push me around, or literally kill me. No more, I determined. No more cowering.

My weapons lay around me. Immediately after arriving in my tent, I spent my time cleaning and oiling the metal of my guns and blades. The action had an odd calming effect on me. I would have preferred a girlfriend or even a puppy or a living breathing creature to experience my affection, but caring for something, even a weapon soothed a part of my soul. Deep inside, I wanted to understand that last vision that I had of Abigail and The Specter.

Once everything was cleaned, oiled, loaded, and ready, I stood up and strapped on my blades and firearms. Two weeks ago, I had never even fired a gun. As I was considering the changes in me and debated whether it was for the better or if I was turning into a monster, a scream from a sentry cut through my thoughts.

I then heard Scott, the camp's smartass, cuss in a manner that only he could muster. Scott was a man in his mid fifties who had the quick smart assed mouth of a sixteen year old. Most people get their asses kicked and learn not to insult others by his age. Not Scott. He had a slightly chubby, goofy appearance, but had a heart of gold for friends and a violent streak that he extended to anyone who would threaten his comrades.

I then heard a scream from a ravaged throat, "I need...speak to Eric."

I didn't recognise the voice, but the throat that issued the request to see me didn't sound human. I was both fearful and curious to see what the creature was that issued that demand.

I fully secured my sword and rifle and burst out of the hootch. Scott stood over a black cloaked and hooded figure that had fallen to the ground from a blow from Scott's Louisville Slugger. He raised his bat and the sentry beside him raised a sword. Together they smashed and stabbed the vampire again.

"Abigail." I murmured with a tinge of guilt, worried that it was her who was seeking refuge in our camp. She would be put to death if she remained at the caverns, and in my madness, I had abandoned her.

"No! Stop!" I screamed as they raised their weapons for the coup de grace. "It's daylight. Vampires are practically harmless now."

They both stopped and glared at me as I rushed up to the form, fearing it was Abigail.

"Abigail," I said as I ran to the pitiful figure.

"What's with you Eric?" Scott demanded. "You want a vamp moving into our camp here. That will definitely bring down the property value in this highclass boardwalk of tarps tents."

No, Scott never made much sense, but despite the odd humor in his words, he was as terrified of the vampire as was the sentry with the sword. Vampires were deadly, capable of mass hypnosis, not to mention the ever present fear of their disease.

Pushing through them, I rushed up and saw the blood leaking heavily, staining the black cloak even darker. I hoped I was in time to save Abigail. I was about to touch her to give care when I suddenly stopped and backtracked in horror.

The pitiful creature looked up at me using its sun blistered hand to shield the daylight from its hideous face, and I instinctively let out a scream of surprise. Its eyes wept a clear, pinkish fluid. Its face was ripped with gashes from the fingernails of its victims. It was hideous, smelly from foul or nonexistent hygiene, and was definitely not Abigail. In its wretched state, I couldn't determine its sex. It might have been male based on the lower voice, but the voice was less masculine than it was hoarse, guttural, and degenerate.

"Please. No hurt. Eric, help me," it pleaded.

"Who are you?" I demanded as I stepped between Scott and the young man with the sword. Although I pitied it, I was also on edge with worry about Abigail.

"Roland," he claimed through a sputtering mess of drooling phlegm.

"I don't care about your name, I want to know--" I stopped talking as I studied its face. I blurted, "You are a failed vampire." It just stared stupidly at me. "What are you doing here? In a camp of humans in broad daylight? Are you insane? How are you speaking clearly?"

"No. I now sane. The Mind dead. The Nunnehi cut off psionic power. Lost control of some of us," he said. "I getting better in the head. Abigail need your help, Eric, savior."

"You're damn right you lost control, walkin' into a human village during the day," Scott said with disgust.

"No. They, The Specter, are losing control of us," Roland said.

"Why are you here, Roland?" I asked.

"A-bi-gail needs you."

"Why?" I asked.

"Specter tooken her to Craigsville," he said with alarm and wrecked English.

"Why?" I asked again.

"Execution. Crucifixion," he blurted.

"Crucifixion?" I asked incredulously. "That's barbaric!"

"She scapegoat for all human deaths," Roland stammered.

"Why? Why would he kill her?" I prompted.

"Because she's good. I good too. Not want to be vampire now."

"Too late for that blood sucker!" Scott yelled.

Scott's bat was still raised to smash its riddled brain. I stayed his hand and he lowered the bat, slightly.

"You must save Abigail," the vampire said. "She die tonight. She fulfills whispered vampire prophecy. There is also the one who will end all pesti– pestilen– disease."

"Why didn't she contact me, through the mind? Telepathy?"

"Psychics no work. The Mind dead. Nunnehi mad. We cut off. We free, if can escape," it said. "But all ends if Abigail killed in Craigtown. You must go there and stop. Save."

"What can I do?" I asked overwhelmed by the task of going into a foreign village and trying to free a vampire from an enraged human lynch mob that numbered at least a thousand strong. I would likely join her on a cross if I attempted to rescue her.

"Finish me," it pleaded. "I dying. Not want to be vampire anymore."

"No," I started to say, but Scott was already in action fueled by his terror, despite the poor condition and friendliness of the vampire.

"OK. Your wish bloodsucker," said Scott.

"No!" I screamed at him again as his bat crashed down on the vampire's skull with a sickening crunch.

"Thank you," the vampire barely croaked as it collapsed from its knees to a prone heap.

Scott reflexively delivered a coup de grace with a crashing smash to the vampire's head. The vampire then twitched a few times and lay still. It was brutal, but everyone feared vampires whether it was daylight or night after what we had been through. Scott still had terror on his face as he nervously looked around in case any other vampires were on the lurk.

I swore. I lifted up the hood and looked at the face that was further distorted from the large indentation into its skull. It was hard to kill a vampire, but a smashed skull was definitely one way.

I swore again and pushed its head away from me. I had to rally the Mountain Warriors to join me. Despite or maybe because of my callous and regretful actions last night, I suddenly felt compelled to save the vampiress at all cost. If need be, I was ready to give my own life in her place. I owed her that. Nothing could stop me.

"Kill, Kill, Kill," David's voice still chanted so softly that I almost forgot its presence.

I looked around the tribe and saw Bryan standing outside his hootch, staring at us with his sword in hand. When he saw that the failed vampire was dead he said, "Bury its body at least one hundred yards outside of the camp."

Everyone in the camp, about fifty members, stared at us. No one dared to get within fifty yards of the dead vampire other than Scott, the sword wielding youth, and me..

"My old ass ain't carrying that thing," Scott said.

I thought that was funny , despite my dark mood. Regardless of being in his mid fifties and getting around with a chronic limp, Scott had little problem keeping up on combat expeditions. The big man would have had no problem dragging the dead vampire. Despite his fearless bluster, I knew that he still feared the dead thing at his feet.

Scott stepped back from the vampire with an even greater pronounced limp from the adventure from the two nights before when we chased the vampires back to their lair. Two younger men grabbed the cloak of the vampire, careful to avoid touching its blood and began to drag it away. Another man followed with a shovel. Bryan observed briefly and then turned back and limped inside the entry flap of his tarp tent.

I realized that Abigail needed us. That she was being led to her death at this very moment. I should have escaped into the woods with her last night as she stood at my side. I also realized that I needed Abigail in a way that I couldn't explain. I was nearly overwhelmed with guilt for threatening to kill her after all she did to help us. When I left her last night, I didn't realize that she had singlehandedly rescued Bradley. That would definitely put her at odds with The Specter.

I instinctively checked to see that my swords and firearms were still secured, and I marched to Bryan's hootch. I rapped the knuckle of my pointer finger on the taut fabric making the sound of a drum. When Bryan bid me to enter, I complied. As soon my eyes adjusted to the internal darkness of the tent, I startled.

Adam sat cross legged, sipping tea, behind a small fire in the tent. From the scent, I guessed the tear to be made of some wildcrafted local herbs. He ignored my presence and stared into the glowing coals that smoldered in a hole in the ground as somber as his eyes that burned equally hot. The smoke rose lazily to the small opening at the top of the tarp teepee. Adam slowly looked up at me. Before he could say anything, I said, "Listen, I'm sorry for my earlier actions, but I refuse to be treated the way this camp has been treating me."

Bryan and Adam looked at each other and then at me. Both were about to answer me when I continued, "Abigail is being taken to Craigsville by The Specter to be executed for all the aid that she has given us. We need to rescue her."

"Out of the question," said Adam.

"It's only right!" I retorted. "She rescued Bradley. The rest of us as well!"

Bryan shook his head and agreed with the older man, "We have nobody ready to go. Those who went to the caverns are still recovering. Hell, this leg wound will have me laid up for another week at least."

He wasn't lying. Bryan was no coward and he paid his debts.

"Then I'll go myself," I proclaimed.

Bryan raised his hand to protest, but Adam looked up at me from under black, graying brows as heavy as thunderheads. He raised his head and glared at me with eyes now hidden by his glasses that reflected the flickering fire light, "Do what you must, but you are on your own, Eric."

I glared at them. I expected Adam to castigate me for my earlier actions. When nothing occurred, I then nodded. I felt my shoulders slump in the resignation that I was indeed alone, but my eyes blazed as I turned to exit the hootch. "Then I'll take my leave, cowards," I said firmly.

"Eric," Bryan called.

"Yes?" I said as I looked over my shoulder at him.

"When Critter gets back he will probably agree to go with you. You know him. He loves a mad adventure." Bryan said. "I'm anticipating that he will be back shortly. You should wait."

"I'll be long gone. She needs me now."

Again I turned to go, but Adam called me back.

"Yes sir," I said respectfully in a pointless attempt to get back into his good graces.

He smashed his lips together as if he believed that my addressing him with respect wasn't sincere and a sarcastic dig. He then said, "We need to talk about the strange and repellant visitors who come to visit you in our camp."

"Who?" I asked.

"The vampiress, Abigail, for one and now that pitiful thing that Scott put out of its misery," he said. "These weird creatures are not welcomed here and you should not associate with them if you wish to remain with us."

I was about to argue, but instead I told him, "I hear you, sir."

They said nothing further. No goodbyes, no wishes for good luck.

With that, I set out on my journey to save the woman I had sworn to kill just a few hours before. As I exited, the villagers looked surprised to see me still ambulatory. I guess they had been expecting Adam and Bryan to deal harshly with me. I had a feeling that the two chiefs were happy to see me leave on a mission that would most likely lead to my death.

| 6 |

A Blackhawk helicopter flew The Specter into Craigsville with a few vampires including a tightly bound Abigail. Upon landing, The Specter immediately marched with his prisoner and entourage of vampires composed of Richard, Lucian, Emily, and the newly turned Dexter to the old southern gothic mansion that served as the headquarters for the town's leaders. The skeletal faced masked man entered the headquarters for the town's seat of power as if he owned it, which he did. None of the human guards challenged him. They only saluted. He pushed his way into Commander Craig's office without knocking as The Specter was the true power in the region.

The Specter and the vampires stopped in the doorway and glared at the pitiful sight. The ruler of Craigsville lay on the floor, writhing in pain from withdrawal symptoms.

"Oh come on! Get off your ass and take your medicine, Craig," The Specter said with a low rumbling chuckle.

Craig crawled to his desk under the disgusted glares of the vampires. Dexter smiled brightly at Craig's predicament. He vaguely remembered meeting Craig when he was still a human scientist not long ago. Craig had been a bit of a smug jackass then. Some of Craig's arrogance was natural, but a good portion of it was fueled by the drug.

From the floor, Craig picked up his golden goblet of golden honey wine that sat on the ground next to him. He swirled the contents and saw the white, undissolved sediment at the bottom. Craig wasn't addicted to it but rather enslaved. In fact, The Specter told him that he would probably die without the drug. The insidious addictive nature was that awful. It was a designer mix of a narcotic and an amphetamine. The Specter knew all this and relished it. It was an unnamed drug to which The Specter had Craig hooked and gave the man-monster control over the commander. From the floor, Craig painfully gripped the goblet in his shaking fist. Commander Craig shot a glance at his .45 caliber handgun that rested on the edge of his desk. The intensity in his eyes betrayed his thought: one shot and it would all be over.

The Specter laughed again. This time it was an actual and rare belly laugh. "Why put yourself through this in front of me? If I were you, I would want to appear in my prime before me. Not writhing like a worm in the sunlight."

Craig mustered up all his strength and shifted his glare from the goblet of the wonderful poison to The Specter. He choked out, "I didn't know that you were coming."

Craig's pain became his world. He had been unable to hear the military chopper as aural hallucinations of screams from the pits of hell in his tormented mind. He felt the mental anguish of withdrawal as vivid as the physical pain mixed with realistic, yet surreal nightmarish visions.

"As well you shouldn't know of my whereabouts," The Specter sighed heavily and said, "Just drink it," he said as he pushed the goblet toward Craig's quivering mouth.

With shaky hands, Craig slammed the liquid down his throat purposely trying not to enjoy the sweet sour mead and the bitter bite of the unknown drug that he had come to crave. Whether it was psychological or if the drug worked that quickly, he didn't know, but immediately, Craig felt the pain begin to leave his body and strength return as if the poison was absorbed instantly through the membrane of his mouth. He pushed himself up slightly from his nearly supine position and looked to The Specter now feeling nothing but love, gratitude, and an odd sense of loyalty for giving him the feeling of immortality, if only for a few hours that the drug affected him. Craig came to his knees and rolled his shoulders back.

"Now that you are feeling better," The Specter said, "We need to hold a trial for our pretty little traitor here. She is responsible for the rash of deaths and giving our vampire friends a bad name."

Craig slowly got to his hands and knees to stand. He felt his arteries invigorated as if by new blood as he unfolded himself as he stood. As he came erect, he rolled his shoulders again and flexed his powerful muscles as he faced The Specter. Craig felt in his prime, even better, and his feelings for The Specter suddenly went beyond mere loyalty. Craig now genuinely loved his masked master.

"When do you want the trial, sir?" Craig asked.

The Specter replied, "Immediately. We need to find her guilty and begin her execution process by evening."

"A shame. She is such a beauty." said Craig as he pinched Abigail's cheek.

Bound and almost helpless, Abigail snapped her teeth trying to bite Craigs hand.

He barely moved his fingers away from her flashing fangs. "I love her. So feisty," he said as he backhanded her cheek, careful to avoid the infected fangs, causing her head to whiplash.

"I want a public trial," said The Specter. "I want all the town folks, every single one, to witness that we are killing the one responsible for giving the vampires a bad name."

"We have a large field in front of the mansion," Craig offered.

"No," The Specter roared. "It must be inside."

"Why?" asked Craig who winced as he expected retaliation for questioning his master.

The Specter didn't resort to violence but rather impatiently explained, "These are vampires. They dislike the sunlight, idiot, even with hooded cloaks. It kills them."

"Then it will torture our pretty little criminal." Craig said.

"No!" said The Specter with finality. "What about the high school gymnasium?"

Craig looked at the ceiling as he did the math in his head, taking in account the space versus current population. "That will work. We have less people still alive these days. We can cram them all in, but it will break the fire code," he added with a grin at the attempted humor. No one gave a damn about the past regulations these days.

The Specter looked satisfied as he said, "Good. Send your soldiers to tell everyone, and I mean everyone, to gather in the gymnasium immediately. The trial will begin within the hour, but first..."

Abigail shuddered as The Specter turned and grinned at her.

"Restrain and hold her well, very tight," The Specter ordered. "Not you Richard. I need you to do something for me."

"Yes master," Richard stammered.

"We need her to be nice and compliant," The Specter said with a cruel gleam in his eyes and a rare smile on his skeletal mask that moved with his facial muscles.

Lucian and Dexter grabbed Abigail's bound arms and held her tight. Dexter smiled with a smarmy look of victory. He had tried to sexually assault Abigail a few hours before she almost killed him. He spoke nothing aloud. His smile said it all.

Once Abigail was firmly secured by the two vampires, The Specter turned to Richard and said, "Withdraw your dagger, vampire."

"No!" Abigail said in sudden panic as she realized what he had planned for her. She resisted against the rough hands and the cords that held her causing her ribcage to spasm as if on fire.

"Specter?" Richard asked hesitantly.

"Do it now!" he bellowed. "And get out your chalice. May as well not waste her blood."

Richard pulled out a long dagger that was thinner than his long boney pinkie finger, but otherwise he didn't move.

The Specter grabbed him by the back of his hooded cloak, pushed him toward his favorite vampiric daughter, and smacked him on the back of his skull. "Now!" The Specter bellowed painfully loud for Richard.

Richard blinked as determination welled up inside of him to follow his master's orders.

"No!" Abigail screamed again as she tensed against Dexter's and Lucian's grip.

Richard mouthed silently, "Sorry, Abigail," careful that The Specter didn't see his apology.

He approached Abigail and quickly but expertly sank his dagger into her neck, piercing her carotid artery. He withdrew the double edged blade and expertly caught her blood into an extremely large golden goblet procured from his black cloak. The other vampires held Abigail up and kept her standing as her strength quickly bled away.

Richard held the goblet until the last spurts of blood turned into a trickle and continued to hold it until the last drop appeared. He then ran the edge of the cup up her graceful neck to catch every last smear of the vampiress' blood. Only when he pulled the goblet away did the other vampires let her collapse in a heap onto the floor.

Lacking most of her blood, Abigail could only weakly look up from her crumpled position. She then watched Richard, her father by the bite, drink a few gulps of her blood. He then passed the cup to Lucian who quickly drank. Next it was passed to Dexter, who leered at her as he indulged and savored her blood, swishing it around his mouth.

She watched this as she lay helplessly on the floor aware that she could not escape her fate now. She had no strength to resist and she was in a town surrounded by thousands of her sworn enemies. She couldn't even use psychic power to get help.

Even without the execution, she would be dead by midnight from blood loss. Abigail began to accept her fate, and said a prayer to her maker, aware of the silver necklace that burned a cross-shaped patch of inflamed skin between her breasts from the vampiric reaction with silver.

| 7 |

I jogged up the steep inclines of the trail and then when fatigued, I walked at a brisk pace toward Craigville. I had only been there once before and my arrival had been in a Madmax looking van with a souped up engine, oversized tires, and gunports bristling with spikes that traveled unstoppable and rapidly over the highways far from my current trail high in the mountains. Later, my running escape had been through a nighttime forest, led by Critter. I now feared that I may get lost in the mountainous wilderness of a seemingly endless forest.

The direction that I was heading now went over the mountain range through a dark forest. I had traveled that route by night following Critter's memory and unerring sense of direction. Now it was a lot of guesswork. I worried about taking a wrong turn because getting lost would mean missing my chance to rescue Abigail, if I even could. Against all of

Craigsville, I was facing odds of about one thousand enemies alone.

Regardless, I persevered onward. Despite the worry, deep in my heart, I had confidence that I wouldn't get lost somewhere. I felt an odd link with the vampiress even with the psionics cut. I trusted that would lead me to her and I offered brief prayers throughout my run that my gut instinct would be correct.

My breath was heavy and my leg muscles burned, especially up the steep inclines, but the workout that the Mountain Warriors had put me through had toughened me beyond what I thought was possible. Although tired and breathing heavily, I felt a reserve of energy that seemed endless. The run actually invigorated me. The scenery was also inspiring as I jogged along sheer rock faces, peered over precipices, and just followed the trail. Just a week ago all this would have terrified me. Now the wild beauty was a balm against the storm toward where I raced. Like Abigail, I came to fear human habitations as much as anything stalking the woods, zombies or vampires.

I crested a ridge and ran along it. I soon found myself in the vampire's killing field. This was where Craigsville sent their condemned prisoners to be fed to the vampires. Many innocent people and petty criminals were wrongly convicted by Craig to feed these monsters, under The Specter's insidious orders of course.

My path cut right through the heart of it, and like the first time I was almost overwhelmed by the quantity of dead human bodies strewn along the trail like empty liquor bottles along the street of a rough neighborhood. Even the scavengers like vultures and raccoons avoided these almost mummified bodies. In the daylight the sight was less creepy than coming upon this death zone at night. However I could see the ghastly distorted faces discolored from decay and blood loss even more clearly.

I did recognize one of the dead who was propped up, leaning against a tree with his mouth opened wide in his final scream. I had never actually met him while he had been alive. I had only seen him when I squatted next to his body while hiding from the vampires. Although I had never talked to him in person, his face had been permanently engraved on my psyche as the now silent scream was forever branded on his face. It was almost as if he was calling on me to personally avenge his death. I had vowed to one day make good on that unspoken plea..

The stench of human rot wasn't as gut wrenching with the cold as it would be in the sweltering summer. For that I was grateful.

I kept my eyes off the dead as much as I could. I couldn't do anything for them now, so I pushed on and was relieved as I left the killing field behind.

I continued to run along the ridge and I felt my gut tighten as I came to a bend in the trail. I felt that destiny awaited around the corner.

I rounded it and found myself on the other side of the ridge on a high cliff. I caught my breath as I saw Craigsvilled down below, nestled in the valley laying out like a rug beneath me. It looked so small and insignificant, like a sparrow's nest in the rafters of a large barn. However, in the valley below awaited a good chance of Abigail and I meeting our end.

For a moment, I hesitated. I could back out and no one would know or blame me for avoiding this impossible task ahead. Actually seeing the town took away my confidence, for a moment, but I knew that I could never forgive myself. I owed Abigail.

However, like the buzz of an annoying mosquito, I heard the whine of a drone ten feet above me and thirty feet away. If The Specter was indeed behind this latest dangerous predicament involving Abigail, he would know that I was heading in his direction. It angered me that even if he did know, he probably wouldn't care. I knew that he saw me as nothing more than a worm. He had called me such. Angrily, I shot the drone with the middle finger and then began running my descent down the mountain.

***

Back at the camp of the Mountain Warriors, the three young men finished kicking the last remaining dirt clods over the grave of the failed vampire that Scott dispatched with his Louisville slugger. As they stood up, straightening their sore shoulders and backs, they were suddenly aware of a fourth man standing in their midsts. They startled for a moment fearing the wrath of Bryan for their inattentiveness. The failure to stay alert for intruders placed the entire tribe at risk.

Bryan saw his tribe as not just his responsibility, but also as his family. Bryan could be quite brutal when defending those he loved, even if the perpetrators were the fellow tribesmen who he was trying to protect.

However the three men relaxed slightly when they saw that it was Critter who had sneaked in among them.

Critter, the woodsman among outdoorsmen, smiled wryly at their startled faces. He enjoyed using his stealth to quietly sneak up and insinuate himself among others. A self proclaimed half redneck/half Cherokee, his tall frame could hide better than people a foot shorter than himself as if by magic.

They looked him over and saw that he carried a gutted groundhog in his hand. The heart, liver, kidneys, and anything else of nutritional or utility value would be in a plastic bag in his small backpack slung over one shoulder. The tracker only shouldered one strap in case he ever had to ditch it for quick combat.

"Relax," he drawled. Critter looked over the newly covered mound and observed, "I guess that this hole wasn't for a tribal member due to the lack of a marker and the mound isn't too high, suggesting a shallow grave."

"Yes, sir," said a short stocky man named Guy. The other two youths were as taciturn as Critter usually appeared. Maybe more so in the presence of one of the three warchiefs of the tribe.

"Zombie?" Critter asked.

"Vampire," Guy said.

"Vampire?" Critter asked with a hint of alarm. "In the daylight?"

Guy nodded and said, "It came to tell Eric that Abigail is in trouble."

"Why isn't ole Eric burying it? It's his friend after all," Critter asked in a humorous tone and a granite face.

"He set off to rescue the vampiress. The Specter is taking her to Craigsville for crucifixion. She's a scapegoat for all the vampiric killings in that town."

"Bullshit!" Critter exclaimed in a rare outburst. "She saved my ass at least two times! Did Eric leave yet?"

"About an hour ago."

"How did he pull that off? Who went with him?" Critter asked.

"No one," Guy said as the other two men looked down as if they were suddenly interested in the newly covered grave.

"What?"

"He lost his mind," Guy said and then told Critter about Eric attacking Adam and demanding respect. "Nobody got near Eric after that. They just let him leave on his own. I think they're glad to be rid of him. Only Bryan and Scott really talked to him and they were mostly friendly despite Eric knocking out Adam."

Critter's normally dour face split into a grin. He usually saved a smile for the times his life was at stake, finding joy in the adrenaline rush, but he did find joy in this news. The woodsman enjoyed the freedom of the wilderness. He also admired the freedom that stirs in the wild beating hearts of the strong.

"Good for him," Critter said to the surprise of the men. The two quiet grave diggers looked up briefly from the dirt as Critter continued, "I knew it was a matter of time before he stood up for himself. I saw those fires blazing in his eyes when we first met. I wondered when it would finally erupt."

Critter's smile left and he stared distantly over the mountains.

"Yeah we–" one of the quieter men began to say.

But Critter was already walking to Bryan's hootch. His jaw had a determined set.

Critter made his way, knocked, and entered as Bryan invited him inside. Bryan was the only one inside.

"Got a gift," Critter said, handing the carcass of the groundhog to Bryan.

"Thanks. You cooking it?" Bryan asked.

"No you can," Critter replied as he pulled a bloody Zip Lock baggie from his pocket. "Also here are the organs, but I will keep the liver, I need to eat it fast."

"What's up?" asked Bryan, who already knew the answer.

"I'm feeling incredibly stupid today," Critter said. "I think I'll follow Eric on a mad adventure."

Bryan nodded and after a brief conversation, Critter finally said, "I will be taking off, now."

"You're saving the vampiress?" Bryan asked.

"If I can. Vampire or not I owe her our lives."

"Impossible," Bryan replied. "But you will reduce the odds of one thousand to one against Eric, to five hundred to one against the two of you," Bryan added with a grim smile.

Critter replied. "Then I'll stop Eric on his fool's mission. If not that, I'll see about turning Craigsville against Craig and The Specter."

"Josh is out of the picture, you know that."

"There might still be a way," Critter said.

"I wish I could join, but my leg isn't worth much today."

"Get well my friend," Critter said with sincerity. He knew despite the odds, Bryan would go with him if able. Although they had fought against the town in territorial disputes, both men had lifelong friends in the town and wanted to see them free of Craig and the puppet master who was The Specter.

"Thanks. Take care my brother," both men nodded solemnly to each other.

As he ate the raw liver, Critter set off on a light jog in a different direction than Eric had taken. He knew all the shortcuts through the rugged wooded mountains. His hope was to get to Craigsville and stop Eric before entering the town, or at least devise a plan. Eric's impulsive nature would get him killed one day, Critter thought as he simultaneously admired the man's spirit.

***

In the Safe Zone, a few dozen miles from the razor wired boundary of the quarantined Forbidden Zone, Tommy Laurens had zoned out watching the footage from the drones. He leaned forward in his plush leather chair with his chin resting in the crux of his thumb and forefinger. His eyes focused with laser-like intensity on the screens as he watched Eric flip off the camera.

He smiled, proud of his friend's defiant nature.

He blinked as a buzzing sound pierced his brain and interrupted his concentration. He looked with confusion at the source of the annoying sound that emanated from behind his laptop. He grabbed his phone and felt excited when he saw that he received a text message from Dexter.

Abigail, the vampiress, had attempted to kill Dexter by drinking his blood to give the appearance that he had been killed by a pack of failed psychotic vampires. The equally psychotic Dexter deserved it. With his scientific skills, only matched by his perverse nature, Dexter had developed a radio controlled army of zombie bots for The Specter. Yes he deserved his death, but Dexter was also a powerful ally to have in these trying times.

But Tommy had sent three soldiers from Craigsville to revive him with a blood transfusion. As soon as he regained his strength, Dexter wantonly killed his saviors. He didn't need their blood. It was a sickening and gratuitous triple homicide. A crime that he would never be held accountable for with the current regime.

Tommy worried that Dexter had lost his mind, but it was common for newly changed vampires to react with such violence. Even Abigail had killed the human who had betrayed her when she awoke after the bite and changed into a vampire, but that was simply to satisfy the need. Dexter, on the other hand, had had a blood transfusion and he certainly didn't need to kill even one of the soldiers for the blood.

It shouldn't have been too big of a surprise. Dexter had a very deviant and perverse nature. He was also a master of the sciences. His job had been to install chips into the brains of zombies so that they could be controlled as soldiers for the regime. He also programmed zombies to be his sex slaves, off the records of course. That last part was definitely not on his job description, but he was indispensable and given many leeways.

Way too much leeway.

Tommy had resurrected him after Abigail had left him for dead in hopes that Dexter would become a powerful ally inside the Forbidden Zone and a protector for his friend Eric, but so far Dexter had not returned any of his texts and phone calls to him. Granted, most cell reception and internet was cut off in the Forbidden Zone, but Dexter was one of the few inside who was given full access to the web.

Just five minutes ago, Tommy had sent his fifteenth text, "Please reply. I saved your life. I need you to help me if you can. If you can take my friend Eric into your protection, I would greatly appreciate it, and I will see what I can do for you from outside of the Forbidden Zone."

With the help of his Uncle, The former governor, Daniel Hildebrande, Eric was supposed to be safely ensconced under the protection of Craigsville. Originally Tommy's goal was to get a reality show based on the survival of the quaint small town that had the protection of full security police force, but by mistake Eric had been captured by the Mountain Warriors who survived in the wilds of the brutal Forbidden Zone. Craigsville was in the Forbidden Zone, but along with the security force, a population around one thousand, and a self-sufficient farming system, they also had a ten foot high wall that surrounded them and afforded them great protection against the zombie hordes.

The Mountain Warriors, on the other hand, survived by constantly battling the elements around them in a simple, nomadic camp. They were fierce but they also lived by a code that tentatively linked them to the civilized world. In many conflicts between rival tribes, the victor would kill every man, woman, and child of the defeated, so they couldn't come back and fight them later or continue to compete for resources. The Mountain Warriors were one of the few who gave a little mercy to their vanquished foes.

The Mountain Warriors had also once been marked for extermination by the government, but as long as Eric resided there, they would be safe by order of Governor Hildebrande. Now the assurance for both Eric and the tribe of the Mountain Warriors was gone with the deposition of Governor Hildebrande.

Shortly after arriving in the Forbidden Zone, Eric had been taken by force to the safety of Craigsville to fulfill Tommy's plan, but had promptly escaped. Living with the Mountain Warriors gave Tommy a great show (the Mountain Warriors lived a far more exciting life,) but Tommy still feared for his friend.

With excitement, Tommy clicked on the message from Dexter.

"Finally," Tommy muttered as the message popped into view..

His facial muscles sank as he read Dexter's message, "Get screwed, Laurens. You need me. I don't need you. I will personally see that Eric will be killed, and by my bite."

"Dammit!" Tommy hissed a curse.

Tommy realized that to save his friend Eric, that he would have to ditch his popular reality show. It wouldn't just cost Tommy his money and fame, but also his status in the government and possibly land him in jail, if he was lucky. The only thing that kept him in good graces with the new regime was that he was pulling in a ton of cash that went into the coffers of the intelligence agency.

However Eric's actions were threatening everything, but damn, Tommy had to admit, Eric was doing what he saw as right, despite going against the odds.

| 8 |

I guessed with the cutbacks that I was within thirty to forty five minutes away from the outskirts of Craigsville. I quickly dismissed my desire to leave the trail and cut straight down the mountain side. It would have been a mile or two shorter, but the hill was insanely steep and heavy with thorny brush. Instead, I stuck with the path and easily coasted down the decline. My breathing returned to normal as I just let gravity power my running stride. Physically, I felt great. I was ready for anything.

I cruised around another bend and stopped suddenly on my path. Ahead of me stood a small horde of zombies, probably about ten of them. They were temporarily immobile in their sleep mode waiting for some noise or scent to rouse them to their ravenous hunger.

I no longer feared them as much as I had in the past. They were stupid and predictable. Although they had no fear of weapons, they were still overpowering in large numbers because they had no hesitation when attacking a man swinging a sword or shooting a rifle at them. In fact the thunderous blast of gunfire only seemed to fire up their savage natures, and they could easily inundate you, surround you, and render your weapons useless. They were driven only by an insane desire for fresh human flesh. Facing ten alone was potentially deadly for me. It may sound easy to fight, but to see that many hungrily charging you as they ignore your bullets or blades ravaging their flesh can test the steel of any warrior. I also didn't want the stench of their rotting flesh on me or my swords.

The fear of their scent on me was probably my biggest worry. That struck me as funny, because a couple weeks ago, I wasn't sure if I was brave enough to even kill one of them.

I was tempted to simply sneak into the woods off the sandy trail and simply avoid them. However, as I stepped off the trail into the dry leaves, I saw a couple of their heads shoot up from the crunching sound made by my boots on the leaves. I held still and they looked straight at me with their vision focusing past me, like goldfish staring unfocused out of a fishbowl. I knew that movement, even a blink of the eye, tended to set them off, but if one held still, they would look right through you as if you were invisible, and eventually go back to sleep. That's if they hadn't already spotted you of course.

I stood my ground, aware that I was wasting precious time to intervene for Abigail. It felt like it was too long of a wait.

My patience was running out for them to return to hibernation mode, but after a long minute or two of rigidly standing still as my body screamed at me to run or fight, they seemed to be nodding off, but suddenly one of their heads shot up. I saw his nostrils flare, and he looked in my general direction.

I knew that he smelled human flesh. A few others did the same until the first one looked straight at me. His dull eyes suddenly cleared.

He roared a hideous shriek through a decomposing throat. The others looked in the direction that he was looking and roared as well when they spotted me. These weren't the rotters that shambled with degenerating muscles. They all had a full set of teeth with no missing spaces from old zombie decay. These had recently turned and were well preserved and virile.

As one, the ten of them sprinted at me. I was done waiting. My sword cleared the scabbard with a razor's hiss of metal on wood and I charged straight into the heart of that mass on the narrow path. They roared and I roared back with an even louder warcry.

As we neared impact, I stepped to the side, slashed, and beheaded two of them with a single stroke. They never ducked, always driven forward with the desire to feed on human flesh with no care or concept of self preservation. I ducked as one reached for me, and I sliced at his thigh, causing him to collapse. I side kicked another's knee and heard a sickening pop of the bone or joint. Those two collapsed onto the trail with the decapitated ones.

I decapitated a fifth. There were still a few more, but I had made my hole in the pack. I ran straight through them like a running back and sprinted down the trail as if heading for a touchdown. I was confident that I could out run them and powered on. I could have killed the rest, but didn't like getting stinking zombie goo on me. Besides unreliable rumors, I hadn't heard of any verified report of a person succumbing to the zombie disease from contact with their blood and gore. Supposedly the pathogen was only transmitted by bite but I never wanted to push my luck and I limited my physical contact with them. I also factored in the ick and the putrid stench of them as a reason for avoiding a fight. I couldn't enter the town with the stench of death on my clothes and attempt to pass unnoticed through the population. Hygiene standards had declined since the fall of civilization, but body odor was nowhere near as intense as the putrid intensity of zombie rot. They smelled far worse than the decomposition of a regular corpse.

I could hear the zombies' cries, shrieks, and snarls fading behind me as I ran. A thrill of victory surged through my heart when the toe of my boot caught a root and I sprawled heavily face first on a large flat rock in the trail. My knee slammed into another stone. Everything in my body felt wrong and I desired to lie there to recuperate, but I heard their snarling approach. I shot to my feet and collapsed as my knee would not support me. I didn't think anything was seriously damaged or broken in my leg. I hoped it was just a temporary shock as my body figured out what happened in the fall.

But I could not call a timeout either. They were rapidly nearing me.

I stood up again, but this time much slower and watched them round a bend about twenty yards behind me. I took off in a shambling run on my injured knee. They were gaining and fast.

I ran in a hobbling shamble and rounded a bend in the trail. I looked and was relieved that I was out of their sight. I half crawled, half climbed up among some boulders above the trail. I scrambled behind one hoping to hide to give my knee a rest as they would forget about seeing me and go back to sleep mode. I watched the small horde pass beneath me and felt a relief spread through my veins, but one of them stopped with her nostrils flaring. The others stopped as well. They followed her gaze, and with a mass roar, they came back toward me when they spotted me in my hide.

I cursed them through gritted teeth, as they scrambled up the rocks to get to me.

I swore loudly and pressed my shoulder on a man sized boulder that was precariously perched above them. They looked at me as the boulder started to give way. There was no comprehension on their snarling faces at what I was trying to do. I put everything I had into pushing it. Hope welled up inside of me as I felt the gravelly sounding groan beneath the boulder, but then the movement of the boulder stopped as the horde continued to run at me.

They kept climbing with clumsy but deadly spastic intensity. One reached around the boulder and I felt his cold and clammy, dead hand on my wrist. A burst of adrenaline from the repulsion of the thing shot through my pulsing arteries and the boulder dislodged and crashed down the mountain crushing a few of them. In retrospect, it was a bit of a noisy plan considering that I was planning on sneaking quietly into town. I didn't watch the boulder as it rolled down the mountain toward the town.

Two zombies remained. I drew my short, two foot long wakizashi sword rather than the large vampiric katana that Abigail had given me. In the rocky lay of the boulders, I didn't have room to wield the larger blade. In all honesty, I drew the wakizashi because that's the first hilt that I grabbed, but sometimes luck seemed on my side.

I sliced off the grabber's arm and then his other arm as he reached for me undeterred by the first amputation. My third slash decapitated him.

Before I could celebrate, a female zombie crashed onto me and we rolled together over the stones. In the crashing roll, I dropped the small sword. The female zombie landed on top of me. Its wretched, smelly drool landed on my cheek as it shrieked and snapped its jaw at my face with my hand on her throat. I gagged at the stench and forced us to roll further downhill, spilling her off of me. She reached for my throat as I grabbed a head sized stone and bashed it into her face. I continued to pound long after she stopped moving. I no longer had the chivalrous apprehension when it came to killing the female undead.

I stood up panting and gathered my swords looking for any remaining zombies. I mercy killed two who had been crushed by the rolling boulder but who were still reaching for me with blazing eyes and snapping jaws. When they were dispatched, I paused, looked, and listened. I could hear the boulder crash into a distant tree far below and then all was silent. Again I scolded myself. Sending it crashing down the hill toward the town that I planned on sneaking into wasn't a great idea in retrospect.

Then I heard a snarl. I looked up the trail to see the zombie whose knee I had shattered followed by the one whose thigh I sliced, round the corner. They crawled after me, single mindedly for my flesh. That oblivion to their own health overpowered by their desire to eat freaked me out more than anything else about them. I limped up the trail and quickly dispatched the two. I knew they were once people with goals, dreams, and loved ones. They deserved a peaceful rest after death. Not the unnatural life of the undead.

Once that was done, I continued on my mission. Each second that passed, my knee felt better. I ran further downhill until I found a small stream tumbling down the steep slope. I went downstream from the trail so that no person following the path would drink what I washed off. I cleaned that sickening slobber off my face with a lot of the homemade hand sanitizer that was made with moonshine, garlic and anything else that the Mountain Warriors could scrounge that had antiseptic properties. I washed it off with copious creek water. Then I wiped the zombie goo off of my swords.

I took off running. With each step I could feel the pain in my knee subside from the movement. I was glad to surmise that it was more from the shock of slamming my bone into stone rather than an actual injury. It would probably hurt like hell later, but hopefully I would have saved Abigail by then or be dead. I thought about the last part in a joking manner. I had to keep my hopes up, even with morbid humor.

I rounded another bend and found myself at the bottom of the valley. I got off the trail and stalked toward the town. I remembered Captain Josh Righter, the head of security lamenting that this end of the town was chronically left under guarded. I prayed that Craigsville was still lax with this area.

I crept and found myself at the wall that was made of everything from barbed wire, old cars and trucks stacked on top of each other, tree trunks, and anything else that could be scavenged for a quick wall. There were no troops within sight. It looked like the boulder that I sent down the hill gathered no attention.

I took the AR-15 off of my shoulder and hid it in an old car that sat at the top of the wall. Unlike the Mountain Warriors where everyone was armed, in Craigsville, only the security force was allowed to carry firearms for fear of awakening a horde of zombies with an errant gunshot. The monsters uncannily followed the sound of gunfire for days. Gunshots usually meant a wounded or dying person, and an easy meal or at least human prey activity.

I kept my swords with me, because quiet weapons including archery equipment were allowed in the town and made sure my handgun was concealed under my coat, holstered in my belt by my appendix. I checked each weapon to confirm that everything was secured and climbed on top of a section of the wall that was eight feet high. It was relatively easy to climb as it was a combination of a rusted six foot high chain link fence with stacked tree trunks behind the length of fence. Once I reached the top, I slid over the edge into Craigsville. I was still in a forested area.

After walking a few meters, I spotted a lone guard as he walked his paces in boredom about fifty yards away. I watched him zip up after he had just relieved his bladder and was walking away from me. He was not expecting a human invader. If a zombie was invading, they didn't take time to hide and would come crashing at him. I had nowhere near the stealth that Critter and Bryan had, but it was enough. I quickly made my way into a small, narrow ditch, and climbed down the bank. The walk was quieter with the stones in the dry creek bed rather than dry leaves under foot.

Stooped over, only my head was above the steep bank, and after a short run through the forest, I found myself on an empty gravel road on the outskirts of a neighborhood. I couldn't help but worry if this was too easy so far.

After walking a few paces on the street, I noticed that I was hunched over as if sneaking. I stood up to full height to avoid making anyone suspicious and confidently walked like I lived there and followed the gravel road with a few houses dotting the rural lane. The headquarters which was the heart of the small town was about a mile away.

Shortly afterwards, I was on a paved road, and then I came upon a huge crowd of people getting directed toward a school gym. I could guess what the main attraction was. I was ordered to join the mob of people by one of the barking security guards in black fatigues.

With a, "Yes sir," I joined the mass of people and marched forward like a townie. From the prodding of the security police to the curiosity of the event, I was paid no heed, but in a small town where everyone at least recognized everyone, I knew that I couldn't rely on blending in for too long. Last time I was here I was practically clean shaven. Now I had a two week beard. I hoped that would help me blend in better. Only the security force members were clean shaven.

I had entered a large high school gymnasium with the crowd. It looked like an angry pep rally with the people crammed into the bleachers and standing on the floor of the basketball court. Everyone was pushed into the stands and ordered to take a seat or packed into the standing area on the floor. I was shoved by the guards into a set of bleachers without being given a choice where I would go. Once in the stands, the guards yelled at us to squeeze together.

I took a seat squeezed between two angry looking men who paid me no mind. Having a vampire on trial had thoroughly captured their attention. I looked toward the front of the gym like those around me. The Specter sat on a large wooden chair that resembled a throne up on the stage behind a raised basket on the court.

"Silence!" the man/monster bellowed in an inhumanly deep gravelly voice after everyone was crammed inside.

A hush came over and I watched a group of fifteen people enter and the crowd parted. Craig pushed Abigail ahead of him as she stopped often. She toppled over after one shove. Abigail could barely walk and looked near death's embrace already with paler skin than I had ever seen, even on a blood hungry vampire. They guided her toward The Specter who stood up to usher in the ceremony. I realized that the whole setup was appropriately on a stage for a staged trial. Lucian, Emily, and Richard and a few other vampires who I didn't recognize somberly followed.

The crowd in the stands mostly watched with silent, dreadful curiosity. However those spectators along the aisle that Craig pushed the vampiress were agitated with rage. These agitators hurled insults and curses at the condemned. Occasionally they would hurl actual objects careful not to hit Craig, the security force, or the other vampires. The contrast between the quiet spectators and the over the top agitators gave the impression of a show trial to anyone, like me, paying attention. I was sure the agitators were either ordered to scream the insults or threatened with violence to do so, but most in attendance appeared like they just wished to go back to their regular lives.

A rock struck Abigail's shoulder and Craig immediately pushed her to the ground. Craig seemed to be purposefully trying to provoke her rage the way he kept shoving and prodding her. I guessed he wanted her to bare her fangs to further fire up the crowd.

I looked to see how the other vampires reacted to having one of their own treated in such a manner. They mostly kept their heads down, especially the usually arrogant Richard. It was as if he had been deflated of his confident air. There was a wiry vampire who kept his head up as if enjoying the proceeding. With a startle, I realized that it was Dexter.

I swore to myself. I suddenly realized that this was the final straw for Abigail's termination. She had killed that sick bastard, but now, he was back and even worse, the sick bastard was now a vampire.

I also noticed that the vampires had flushed cheeks showing that they had recently fed on blood. Only Abigail was white, beyond pale, and her fiery eyes in her sickly pale face betrayed her blood hunger. Enraging her would be an easy task, however she did a good job keeping it together.

I looked at her closely and was alarmed. Her paleness was a deathly pale. For me, her appearance stirred pity. For the crowd, who did not know her personally, she looked dead already, like she should be laying in a coffin, ready to go beneath the grass. Her insipid face contrasted with her sharp eyes gave her a more monstrous appearance to the rowdy crowd. I knew that whatever they did to her to give her that appearance was purposeful.

The vampires and Craig mounted the stairs to the stage and when they were a few feet from The Specter, Craig bowed respectfully as did the vampires to The Specter. Despite her condition and the restraints, Abigail stood as tall as she could. Craig shoved her to her knees, and Abigail flashed him an angry snarl. Besides the other more obvious changes that vampirism induced, vampires were capable of terrifyingly loud shrieks that no human was capable of making. Her snarl clearly unsettled the crowd.

Oh no, I thought, she bared her fangs. The entire crowd, including the spectators who had demonstrated little interest, immediately erupted with boos and taunting jeers. I knew that whatever they did to her to weaken her and give her that pale look also put her into the blood madness that is uncontrollable for most vampires.

"Stand her up so she may face her charges," The Specter demanded.

Craig easily picked her up by the scruff of her neck. He then whacked her on the back of her head. It was too much in her state. Her eyes blazed with inhuman, vampiric fury as she weakly lunged at Craig's throat. When her flashing fangs were within inches of the hard man's soft flesh, The Specter yanked her back by the hair.

Her anger was boundless as she snarled her fury until she met my eyes. Her rage was immediately quenched. Embarrassment and shame settled across her features as she looked in my eyes. The eye contact lasted barely a second before The Specter slammed her to the floor on her chest and knees, but in that moment, I prayed she took comfort in knowing that she had a shred of hope, even if I was simply a friendly face. I am sure she didn't think that I alone could rescue her, but I racked my brain for a rescue plan, even if it all looked hopeless.

From the floor, Abigail glanced at me sharply again, and I didn't hear her in my head like a voice. The psionics had definitely been cut. However a thought entered my head, "Go Eric! You can not save me."

She immediately looked away so as not to give my presence away.

The Specter then addressed the auditorium. "You have been terrorized by monsters, real monsters, for the last two years. The zombies are bad enough, but they are brainless. This creature before us, however, has intelligently stalked you, and even worse, she has given her coven of vampires a bad name. Richard, the leader has been gracious enough to hand her over to us so that, together, we may end this scourge of vampirism."

I looked at Richard as he held his eyes downcast. Usually he was arrogant and aristocratic in action, speech, and stature, but with The Mind dead and the Nunnehi shutting down whatever psionic power they had, Richard looked like any other person. He even looked as broken as his prized pupil who he saw as his daughter in the firm grasp of The Specter.

The Specter continued, "At present she is incapable of speaking as you saw her respond with only the most savage of snarls. Anything from her mouth would be offensive and even blasphemous."

Abigail, struggled to stand and said, "Hold on--"

Craig smacked her head and she fell to the ground without resistance. Her prior rage had sapped her of any remaining strength to stand, but she bared her fangs again causing the agitators in the front to jeer viciously at her.

I reflexively stood up with the more rowdy crowd but sat back in the bleachers as those behind me yelled. "Sit down!" "Get out of the way!" "Dumbass!" With the distraction of the agitators and Abigail's own snarling, no one else had noticed me other than those in the back.

However the passive onlookers were starting to stir. What had long haunted their nightmares, the stalking, vicious vampire of the dark legends, now knelt in chains before them. Her baring her vampiric fangs only prompted their hatred for her. I now heard more curses hurled at her from those who were once silent.

Inside my mind was roiling, but I forced myself to stay calm. Now was not the time to play my hand. I worried that it was cowardice on my part but I told myself that the reason for my delay was that I wanted to see what The Specter was up to. More realistically, there was no way I could save her at the time. It would be suicidal for me to try anything at this moment, even to offer a shouted protest at this sham trial. I would be mobbed if I spoke any words in her defense. I was about to accept my own silence for the time being as those around me shouted demands for her death.

Craig cinched the chain around her neck and brought Abigail up to her knees again from her prone position. It seemed that vampires had bursts of energy that propelled them above human strength and then totally depleted them afterward when they were out of blood. Despite her earlier rebelion, she appeared barely capable of slouching in a kneeling position now as she sat on her heels. Infact, Dexter held her up so she didn't sprawl on the floor as if dead.

The Specter then raised his arms to the sky calling for quiet. "The guilt for her crimes demands punishment. Citizens of Craigsville! Her crimes are against you! You shall determine her fate. Shall it be prison?"

I knew that prison was out of the question. Citizens of Craigsville never faced prison because of the scarcity of food. It was either a death sentence or a slap on the wrist for any punishment. There was no luxury for a punishment between those extremes, and there was no way that they could keep a vampire in jail. I knew it. The Specter knew it.

"No!" shouted the agitators in the front.

The Specter brought his hands to his chest, palms up, as if wishing to physically receive their demands and asked, "What do you demand?"

About twenty agitators in the front demanded as if on cue, "Crucify her!"

The way they demanded the same execution in one voice, shook me to my core, far surpassing the anachronistically brutal nature of the torturous punishment. I could tell that it had been rehearsed before the show trial.

The agitators began to chant, "Crucify her! Crucify her!" Those around me who had appeared only mildly interested, compelled by the agitators, quickly joined in an almost deafening roar. "Crucify her! Crucify her!"

Everyone was now on their feet screaming the chant. I joined in the standing so as not to stick out, but I didn't shout the chant, of course.

The madness of the crowd shot a bolt of fear followed by wavering cowardice through me, but what could I do? Think Eric, I told myself, but overwhelmed with hopelessness and guilt from my actions last night, my brain could not function.

The Specter raised his arms again. Despite the blood madness of the crowd, no one wished to defy The Specter. Instantly, the gymnasium went silent.

"Hear me, people of Craigsville," The Specter proclaimed in an officious tone. "I have heard your decision. Your demand for her method of execution is full of wisdom and justice. What we have feared shall be raised on high so we may see that we have conquered the evil that has plagued us."

He paused dramatically until a shout shattered the stillness. The Specter actually looked startled.

"This is injustice!" a loud voice called from the back of the gymnasium.

I followed everyone else's stare to the man who did what I dared not. He was a scruffy man with a short but wild beard to match his crazy eyes. He wore a soiled black uniform of Craigsville's security force with a bloody bullet hole in the thigh that caused him a slight limp as he approached the stage.

The people of Craigsville, especially the security forces, took pride in their ability to maintain a clean cut appearance in the post apocalypse world. The upstart looked like a madman who would carry a sign proclaiming that, "The end is near," on the streets of New York City.

However, his outburst brought about a void in the proceedings that he promptly filled with more of his words of his protest against the injustice. A man in a hooded black coat tried to hold him back, but gave up. I caught a flash of the hooded man's eyes and I had a moment of deja vu. I could have sworn that I recognized him, but I wasn't sure where. The hooded man had an equally wild beard as the man who interrupted the proceedings. Beneath the coat it looked like he also wore the black uniform of the Craigsville security police. I was sure that wherever I had seen him he had been clean shaven and in control. I scanned my mind of all the people who I had known back in Washington DC, sure that he had to be some kind of operative. In a crowd of unfamiliar faces a slightly recognisable one stood out like a slap in the face. No one else seemed to recognise the hooded man, but the crowd was focused on the man who dared to interrupt The Specter.

The wild man who had interrupted the court shrugged off the grasping hand of the vaguely familiar man and continued to rant, "She saved me when Craig let The Specter deliver me to that brood of the vampires. Without her I would have met the same fate of the other soldiers that he fed to them. The other vampires on the stage are the true criminals, not Abigail."

Richard, Emily, and Lucian stood wide eyed and speechless as Abigail slowly got up from her knees and stood wobbly but defiant. Dexter ran his hand across her shoulder. His slimy demeanor sickened me. He had attempted to sexually assault the vampiress last time I saw him, and I felt a homicidal desire for his blood override my cowardice for a moment.

Craig looked equally stupefied as the vampires and turned his gaze to his master.

The Specter glowered at the wild upstart for a moment before raising his voice.

"Kill that man!" The Specter ordered in his inhumanly deep voice. "He is a deserter!"

As the agitators swarmed the wildman as he called out, "I am Douglas Bircher! I have lived my whole life in this town! Like you, I was betrayed by our drug-addled leader!"

Douglas tried to continue his speech as he was mobbed, "To execute her is an injustice!" His focus was solely on screaming to the crowd, and he didn't try to defend himself as he was quickly beaten to the ground and silenced. The mob, who were made up of the agitators, brutally stomped him into the hardwood floor with combat boots. I was sure that Douglas, whoever he was, was dead from the brutality of the assault.

"Order! Order!" The Specter's voice boomed as the agitators quit beating the poor man and everything immediately quieted down. I caught a glimpse of the familiar looking hooded man, who had tried to restrain Douglas, sneaking out the back door of the gym. I began to suspect who that mystery man was, but he had disappeared from sight.

"Abigail," The Specter proclaimed, "will be crucified until death immediately after the sun sets tonight."

I took in a deep breath and blew it out. I only had a few hours to figure something out. The crowd around me stood still as they cheered The Specter's words. However, feeling rushed, I pushed past the cheering spectators and went for the backdoor trying to appear casual. However, the crowd was riled up to the point where I attracted no attention.

Once I entered the empty halls, I took off in a sprint. I rounded a corner and caught a glimpse of the lone figure down the hall exiting the school building through a set of double glass doors.

"Josh!" I hissed trying to get my voice to carry to him without alerting the whole mob that I had left in the gymnasium. The crowd was cheering at something The Specter had announced, but I was on edge and didn't hear what the skull-faced man man had announced.

Josh didn't respond to my call, but only walked a little quicker as he opened the door. I was certain that he heard but was ignoring me. I followed him through the doors in a hurry.

"Josh!" I hissed again when I was within ten yards of him on the concrete sidewalk outside.

As I rapidly closed in on him, in one fluid motion he turned to face me while drawing a handgun from his waist, keeping it low and somewhat concealed. He pointed the gun at my heart from his hip.

"Whoa, whoa, whoa!" I exclaimed as he brought it up to aim at my head with deadly determination as he looked at my face. I could almost hear the creak of metal as his finger tightened on the trigger. His eyes narrowed with the promise of death.

| 9 |

"It's me, Eric. Eric Hildebrande," I told Josh.

Captain Josh Righter had been head of security barely a week and a half ago. He had given me a tour of Craigsville and had told me that he wanted to overthrow Craig and ultimately The Specter. He had been overheard on a hidden microphone in the cafeteria when he said this and was sentenced to death in the vampires' killing field. He obviously escaped. I knew he was a good hearted man, and I prayed that he felt the same toward me. Despite being a man of good character, he was also a warrior who would kill an enemy without hesitation. Besides a good heart, I also hoped he had the wits not to fire a gun and alert everyone inside of his presence.

Josh squinted at me suspiciously and lowered the barrel of his gun so that it no longer pointed at my face but rather my abdomen. He nervously looked around as if fearful that anyone else would recognise him, but we were alone.

"Eric? The journalist?" he whispered harshly.

"Put the gun away and let's go away from here and talk before we attract attention," I said.

He did another quick scan of the area and holstered his handgun with a violent thrust into his waist holster. "Let's go," he hissed as he turned and jumped down the remaining three front steps of the walkway in front of the school with cat-like agility.

I quickly followed. He led me down a series of alleyways and stopped at a door to an old barn-like structure that looked to serve as a garage to the abandoned, boarded up house in front of it. The old barn was half covered in flaky white paint. The rest of it was exposed, dark gray rotting wood. A padlock locked the large garage door. Josh wanted to go inside.

"I can probably pick that," as I fingered a crude pick and rake that I had fashioned from two paper clips in the last week.

Josh glared at me and rolled his eyes and opened the unlocked smaller door next to the locked one.

I felt like kicking myself. Lock picking was one of the few skills of value that I had in these wastelands and I had a compelling urge to prove to others that I was not just useful but also streetsmart. Instead, in my overenthusiasm to prove myself, I just looked stupid.

I followed him inside, and as I was still scolding myself, he immediately turned and shoved me up against the wall of the questionable structure causing the old frame to shake. I thought that the dilapidated barn would collapse on us for a second. His other hand thrusted the handgun into my face.

"Josh," I said looking in his eyes and not at the black soulless eye of the barrel, "It's me, Eric!"

"I damn well know who you are, Hildebrande! You're the last guy I talked to before I was arrested and fed to those things. No one else heard me discuss those plans that day, but you!"

Anger overwhelmed my fear of the gun as I pushed him away and said, "The chow hall was bugged. You were with me the whole time. I could never have ratted you out even if I wanted to."

He considered me for a moment. His gun was still aimed at my face as he stepped back. I think his greatest fear was getting recognised by anyone else. His eyes were bright and energized with paranoia, quite different from the man who was in full control of the town's security force, not to mention he struck me as a level headed man in control of his base impulses. Now he was a bundle of electrified nerves.

After a moment, some of the crazy light left his eyes as he holstered the gun again as my words in my defense finally got through his jangled nerves.

"What do you want?" he asked, as his fingers lightly tapped the butt of his handgun, ready for a quick draw.

"Same as you and that guy, Douglas Bircher. I want to free Abigail." When he stared at me with slight confusion, I said, "Abigail. The innocent vampiress who Douglas tried to defend."

He spat into the dirt floor of the barn that was stained with ancient motor oil as he said, "I could care less about those vampire freaks! My concern is with Specter and that drug addicted Craig turning my hometown into crap."

I nodded looking for common ground, "Yes, Abigail may not be one of the townsfolk, but she could be a potential and powerful ally if we can rescue her."

He stated angrily rather than asked, "So I am to trust you? You, who were given a cush job to record the life of this town at the betrayal of Bryan and Critter?"

I thought for a moment. When Josh was dragged to the vampires' killing field, I was still in The Specter's good graces and Bryan and Critter, Josh's childhood friends from before the zombie apocalypse, were in a jail cell with him beneath the Craigsville headquarters building. The last time those two talked to Josh, they thought that I had betrayed them.

I eyed him levelly as I told him, "I helped Bryan and Critter escape and we went to rescue you when you were dropped off in the vampire's feeding ground. I witnessed the scope of their killing fields. The three of us battled the vampires and we would have died had not Abigail saved us. There were hundreds of those vampires, and we were on their turf. She saved our asses. I just snuck back into town only an hour ago to rescue her."

Josh nodded. His muscles relaxed and it seemed like the anger physically dropped from his face as an understanding came upon him. He said, "Yes, I heard the sword battle raging behind me as I ran from their killing field that night. I wondered who that was or if the vamps and the zombies were fighting."

"No, that was Critter, Bryan and me after I helped them escape. We were trying to meet up with you."

"I'll be darned. Had I known that, I would have come back and helped. I always liked Critter and Bryan. They're good men."

"They feel the same about you, Josh," I replied.

"So if you escaped this hole, what the hell are you doing back in town?" he asked.

I started from the beginning to give the reason why he should help Abigail. "The Specter kidnapped Bryan's son and took him to the Vampire's Caverns under Shining Rock Mountain. The Mountain Warriors and I attacked the caverns and I got separated and the tribe abandoned me in those caves. Abigail, who was supposed to kill or turn me into a vampire, helped me escape with Bryan's son. Then--"

"Wait. You attacked the vampire's cave system and escaped."

"Yes?" I said not sure where he was going. I purposely showed him my neck to demonstrate that I had no bite marks nor scars.

"Holy cow! I figured you were just some geek reporter. I didn't figure that you had the balls to-- Holy cow! Douglas told me some of that. About the caves. That Mind thing that had control over him."

I nodded and said, "Abigail and I killed it. That's why they're killing her. She also tried to kill Dexter, that mad–"

"--scientist. I know about that sick, perverted bastard. I saw him up there on the stage," he growled.

There was an awkward silence as I could almost hear his brain grinding to reclassify me and hopefully Abigail. Even with evidence, it takes a moment to go from extremes of desiring to kill someone to considering them an ally. He looked me over and then peered into my eyes and said, "You look like a completely different man. I almost didn't recognize you at first." Then he asked, "How the hell did you get back inside the town?"

"I remembered you lamenting the lax security at the North Cove. I simply walked in like I owned the place."

He chuckled ruefully, "Yep, I did the same. I always told them to guard it better. That will change after I depose Craig." He looked over the inside of the barn and laughed again.

"What?" I asked.

"I busted meth heads and other degenerates in this barn when I was on the force, back before it all went down. I never thought that I would be plotting the overthrow of the town's leadership in this very place." He scratched his furry jaw as he scanned the rotted wood that made the ceiling rafters as if considering how he would start a roof repair project in this barn.

He finally pinned me with his commanding stare and asked, "Do you have a plan?"

"Of course," I lied, not wanting to look like a fool rushing in. My plan was simply to look for an opportunity. Now my plan was to follow Josh, "But let's hear your ideas first since you know the place better than I do."

He nodded in agreement, "I'm flying by the seat of my ass too."

I couldn't help but crook my lips in a quick smile. It didn't last long.

Ironically, he said that as we heard a helicopter flying away. Josh said, "Our buddy, Specter, is flying off on his whirly bird broom stick to God knows where. He will be back at dark. I want to get to Craig when the jones for The Specter's drug kicks in. We will keep him out of commision and retake the town. But the first thing I gotta do is clean up."

Josh had a small backpack and pulled out a razor. I cringed as I watched him shave with nothing more than a canteen of water for the lubricant. I was surprised that he didn't knick himself too badly as he shaved off the wildman's beard with the blade. He wiped the razor against his pants legs occasionally to both clean and strop the edge. The facial hair was nowhere near what the Mountain Warriors wore, but I had previously seen him as an impeccably clean cut military leader less than two weeks ago.

He spoke when he could, between swipes with the razor against the skin of his contorting face, and laid out a loose plan. His rough sketch was to reassume his status as the Head of Security and roughly second in command of Craigsville. As he shaved, he explained between making faces how he was going to don his old uniform and simply order his men to do as he commanded. He talked as he kept his main focus on a small signal mirror as he shaved off the beard. As he finished he looked up and saw the incredulous look in my eyes.

"What?" he asked.

"So people will see you in your uniform and instantly obey you?" I asked.

His eyes were firm as he finished, telling me that the answer was, "Yes."

So I made the further point, "Even after you were banished or assumed AWOL from your duty, you think that they will follow your command?"

He nodded and handed me his razor without a word, but the intent in his eyes was clear. I didn't like dry shaving, and even worse, I absolutely hated using someone else's hygiene equipment, but regardless, I got to work with his razor without question.

He answered in a Southern drawl that had become less offensive to my north eastern snobbery the longer I stayed in this region, and he took on an air of a southern gentleman elucidating a theory in a college classroom.

"Uniforms, costumes make a difference. When Napoleon's men met their unfortunate demise in Russia, a jailed General Claude-Francois De Malet acquired a General's uniform and issued forged orders from his cell in a mental institution. The orders proclaimed that Napoleon was dead in Russia. In a uniform, General Malet then declared himself as the new ruler of France and all the major positions of government were filled by his friends. Historians have called it 'the strangest conspiracy ever.' General Malet almost succeeded in just a few hours until someone looked a little closer, and he was quickly executed by firing squad. People follow any orders given confidently by men in costumes. Cops and soldiers are simply men who are just as scared as everyone else, but like actors, we play a part." He paused as he looked wistfully into the rafters and added. "I was working on a novel that was a modern day fictional account of General Malet's coup attempt, before all this crap went down of course."

"You were writing a novel," I asked.

The tone of my voice didn't escape his attention as he asked, "What? You don't think a hillbilly like myself could write a novel based on French history?"

I retorted, "Well, you didn't think a city boy, journalist like myself could survive the Vampire's Caverns."

"Touche," he said with a smile and a shrug.

He pulled out a clean black uniform from his backpack and began to take off his dirty clothes. I turned around to give him some privacy. I had just finished shaving my beard when I felt something made of clothing slap my back. I looked behind me and saw that he had tossed me a black paramilitary uniform.

Josh said, "This was for Douglas. The fool couldn't keep his mouth shut while we were supposed to be doing a silent recon."

I felt a stab of guilt that Douglas took the fall as I stayed silent. What Josh considered foolish, I saw as righteousness that went beyond my own courage.

Josh continued, "Your job is just to look confident like my back up, and of course shoot people if they don't obey me, but only if I shoot first." He said that as he looked at my waist where my handgun was concealed under my coat. Like an observant police officer, he uncannily knew that I was armed. I wanted to ask how I gave away that information, but we had more pressing matters at the moment. I guessed that I was probably standing awkwardly or something.

He also made his lethal statement with no humor so I just nodded instead. I guess I was expecting to see a smirk, a sinister scowl, or something as he gave such a brutal command to shoot others, but he delivered it as if telling me to take out the trash at a restaurant. The Forbidden Zone was a different world and I was just beginning to mentally adjust to it.

We finished dressing. I looked him over in his new uniform and fresh shave. He was right. Just with the quick change of appearance, I was psychologically ready to follow his orders. Besides, his men loved and respected him before he was sentenced to death. He seemed to stand a few inches taller, his confidence covered him almost as tangibly as his fresh uniform and his eyes blazed with the assurance of his command.

I asked, "So where do we go first?"

"The mansion. I have a feeling that Douglas was taken to the dungeon alive. We gotta get him some decent care. Then I am paying that addict Craig a little visit. He will be jonesing for his drugs soon. I got to know his patterns as his Chief of Security. He's very predictable. We will hopefully be able to free Douglas and get a few others to fight with us, hopefully the whole security force."

"So we're just going to waltz right up to the front door and enter the enemy's headquarters?" I asked skeptically.

"No. We'll waltz right underground into the headquarters' basement dungeon. Besides, they aren't all enemies. Most of the soldiers are my friends. I think I can get a good portion of the troops on my side. They will fight with determination under my rallying cry. I don't think the otherside will have the metal to kill their townsfolk for The Specter, or so I hope."

I nodded and then asked, "What do you mean by waltz in 'underground?' I hope you are speaking in metaphorical terms."

I didn't like it when he smiled. After spending almost two days under the Caverns of the vampires, I feared the claustrophobic confines of tunnels.

His smile disappeared and without a verbal reply, he kicked aside a pile of rotting boards on the floor, and pulled out a crowbar from a rusted toolbox and lifted the edge of a steel and concrete hatch. He didn't need it, but I instinctively helped him pull the heavy lid aside.

"Don't pull the grate too far," he grunted,

The hatch was heavy, so I told him not to worry as I let go of it.

"We gotta cover our tracks," he said. "Go ahead," he pointed with his chin to the hole.

I descended ten feet into the hole down a ladder made of ancient rungs that seemed to be more rust than steel, staining my hands an orange red. I waited at the bottom in the mud as he followed. He replaced the grate over the hole. After joining me at the bottom, he then led the way and disappeared into the darkness. I followed the sound of his slow footsteps in the muddy soil. I oddly found myself more claustrophobic here than in the Cavern of the Vampires. Maybe my fear of vampires far exceeded my phobia of caverns, I guessed. Occasionally he flicked on a flashlight and then just as quickly flicked it off.

"This place is pretty cool," he said as he walked in a squat through a rock tunnel that was approximately five and a half feet in diameter.

I didn't voice my disagreement, but in my opinion, cool only described the air temperature of the dank passage.

After walking a few hundred meters, he flicked on the small headlamp and attached it to his head. The weak batteries dimly illuminated a small circle in front of him. Candlelight would have been brighter. After two years in a post zombie apocalypse, fully charged batteries were a luxury.

He stopped at an ancient stone wall and pulled a steel lever. The rock wall opened slowly, creaking in protest. "This was part of the underground railroad back in the 1850s. One side of my family owned slaves. The other side used these tunnels to help them escape before the Civil War. Then these tunnels were later used by moonshiners in my family before and during the Great Depression. The side of my family in law enforcement mostly turned a blind eye. Can't fault a man for providing for his family."

He ducked into the new tunnel and turned off the light to conserve batteries. I didn't duck enough and my face was caught in a mask of cobwebs. I hate spiders almost as much as I hate tunnels in a cave inhabited by vampires. I clawed them away and walked into another thick tapestry of the dusty, creepy silk. I cursed bitterly as some got into my mouth and Josh shushed me with a hiss.

Josh whispered, "Be grateful. Cobwebs are a sign that no one else has passed through here in ages."

"Why would anyone avoid these lovely passages," I asked as I spat out the cobwebs. My teeth crunched on the dust. It was repulsive..

He ignored my sarcasm and instructed me, "But don't get lax down here."

"Don't worry about that," I rasped back as I knocked aside more webs with my handgun.

"And don't get any of that gunk in your handgun. And definitely don't point it at my back!" he said over his shoulder.

I almost said sarcastically, "Yes, mom," but I held my peace as I focused on breathing and staying relaxed and ready. Staying relaxed kept my limbs more agile like springs ready for action rather than rigid stilts.

I guessed that we traveled three hundred yards in total underground, but in the moment, I would have sworn that we covered twenty miles. However long the tunnel was, it was long enough that my socks and boots were damp. Occasionally the mud turned into ankle deep water. I despised wet socks just slightly behind my dislike for spiders in confined spaces.

I could only imagine the terror of trying to escape slavery in this dank passage. Back then, besides black widow spider bites, they had slave masters to worry about. These days we had crazed warlords, zombies and vampires to worry about. I wasn't sure which point in history sucked more.

Josh stopped as we came to a deadend. He flicked on his headlamp, and I was appreciative that he was aware of his flashlight's beam and avoided shining it into my eyes as he turned to me, even if the light was dimmed with ancient batteries.

"Where do we go now?" I asked.

"Through the wall," he said in a quiet but tense tone. "I am not sure who's on the other side so be prepared for battle, but place your gun in the holster and play it cool af first. The men on the other side may be our friends. I'm hoping that they are, at least. Let me do the talking."

I nodded and whispered, "You got it, Captain."

He shot me a quick glance at the slight but unintentional sarcasm I had when I said Captain. I had a thing against authority and titles.

"Sorry," I muttered.

He replied, "I'm not being a hard ass just to be a hard ass, but your submission to me is vitally important for this plan to work."

"Yes sir," I said with a genuinely respectful tone. I knew that he had every reason to be on edge.

The wall pivoted with a creak, and I was greeted with a surprise.

"Abigail," I whispered.

| 10 |

Our eyes met and I resisted shouting her name and rushing to her. Abigail was curled in a ball in the corner of the cell. It was the same small dungeon room that I had occupied on my last visit to Craigsville. It was made of steel cattle panels chained and welded together. A stairway led upwards in the tight confines. The room was lit by a single dim bulb. Despite the gloominess of the dungeon, the rare sight of an electric light brought an odd feeling of hope to me. Something about electricity after living in a primitive environment, really got to me both times that I was here even if the room lived up to its name, "the dungeon."

I looked at the lock on Abigail's cell and was disappointed. It was an Abus lock. It was unpickable due to the configuration of the pins, but I didn't worry. I'd just acquire the key.

Josh and I stood in the small area outside the barred enclosure where a guard would keep watch, but my focus was on Abigail. She was pale from lack of feeding on blood, but a cough occasionally racked her body and I saw a dried spot of her own blood at the corner of her lips from where The Mind had crushed her ribs. It seemed that The Specter and others had roughed her over to be sure that, despite her regenerative powers, the vampiress would surely die this evening whether she was crucified or not. I could tell that she desperately needed blood. Her deep eyes probed into my own and then she gave a sideways glance to her guard.

I looked over and saw the guard raising his gun and pointing it at us. It was the same guy who guarded the cell when I was imprisoned with Critter and Bryan. The last time we met, I knocked the guard unconscious to help Bryan and Critter escape. He was not happy to see me to say the least.

"Lower your gun, Private," Captain Josh Righter commanded in a tone so deep with so much authority that even I felt compelled to obey and he was not talking to me.

"Captain Righter?" the guard said in a shocked reply.

"Of course it's me. Lower the damn gun or I'll court-martial your ass for insubordination!" Josh commanded as he walked toward the barrel pointed at his face with supreme confidence. There was a handgun in Josh's hand, but it was aimed at the floor. He was armed solely with the costume and confidence of authority, not to mention his reputation.

The guard kept the gun up but not with aggression, but rather the shocked look as if seeing a ghost return from the grave. In the guard's shock he lowered the barrel slightly so that it pointed at Josh's chest as he asked, "How did you come through the wall, sir? I thought you were dead. Fed to the vampires," he babbled.

"Get that out of my face! That's a direct order," Josh said as he confidently stepped closer to the guard so the barrel touched his chest and then possessively took away the Private's handgun. Josh then firmly smacked the guard across the face. It looked more like a display of dominance to snap the Private out of his shock, rather than to cause pain or injury.

"Never point your gun at me again or you will be immediately executed for insubordination. Do you understand, Private?" Captain Righter proclaimed with his fists clenched at his side at the level of his belt.

"Yes sir," the guard said quickly and then curiously looked at me but still addressed Captain Josh Righter. "I thought he, Eric Hildebrande, escaped to the Mountain Warriors." The guard scowled as he accused me, "That journalist stole my gun!" he said looking at the handgun in my appendix holster. I had indeed knocked him out when I rescued Bryan and Critter. Bryan took the guard's handgun and then gave it to me.

I remained silent.

"Quit listening to idle gossip at the barracks, kid. He's with me. Now, put this away." Josh ordered as he returned the handgun to the guard.

I wouldn't have given the handgun back to someone who had just pointed it at me with murderous intent, but Captain Josh Righter was making the point that he was indeed in charge and the guard was still a soldier under his command, not a prisoner. The Private holstered the firearm at his hip.

Josh then looked at the cells. Abigail occupied the cell I had been given on my last visit, but I was startled when I realized that the second cell had an occupant this time. It wasn't just because of the lack of light that I hadn't noticed before, but Douglas lay in a broken heap covered with a ratty woolen blanket that blended in with the gray concrete of the floor. Only his pallid, bloody face peeked out from the covering. He looked as if he hadn't moved since he was unceremoniously dumped into the cell. I heard a gasping wheeze from him and I guess that like Abigail, he acquired some broken ribs in his capture and beating. He looked closer to death than she.

"First off, let Douglas out and get him some medical attention immediately," Josh said with a mix of command and tenderness.

The guard just stared at him.

"Now!" Josh boomed. A scarlet fury suddenly masked his face.

"I can't," said the guard.

"That's an order," Josh stepped nose to nose with the guard. The guard looked down under the fierce stare.

The guard muttered, "Then you should know that only Craig and Lieutenant Elmer Ranklin have the keys to the cells now," the guard glanced at me and weakly added, "ever since that escape"

Josh looked at me, "You're on, journalist lockpicker."

I withdrew my homemade paper clip picker and turning tool. It was pointless, even if I had my professional set, but I went to work anyway as I said to Josh, "I'll give it a try, but The Specter knew what he was doing. This one uses small wafers in place of pins. I can usually pick most security pins like spools and–"

Josh swore and with an impotent rage and paced in the cramped, dank area as I pointlessly worked on the lock. He then whipped around to Douglas' cell. Josh squatted and asked the supine man. "Douglas, are you alright, buddy?"

Douglas moaned in pain as he shifted to look at his boss and croaked out between gasping breaths, "They beat me pretty bad, sir."

I kept on working, just to keep myself busy and cringed as I saw the drying blood caked on Douglas's face, especially around his mouth and nose. A bubble of blood inflated from one of his nostrils and popped.

"Hang in there man. We'll get you through this." Josh said as he punched the dripping stone wall with enough force to cause an echo from the impact. I expected his face to wince in pain, but he looked like he simply desired to punch someone in the face rather than a senseless wall of stone.

I got the key hole to turn a fraction and then it stopped with a false set. That's how picking these damned locks went. I smacked the lock angrily, and quit. I squatted in front of Abigail. "How are you?" I asked.

"OK," she said but I knew that she was lying. In the past, I had never seen more zest for life in anyone's eyes besides

Abigail's. She was the opposite of undead, in my opinion, but now her eyes appeared to be slowly dimming like the last flickers of a used up candle.

"Baloney! You look near death. What did they do to you?" I asked

She took a deep breath hesitant to say anything and then said, "They drained me of my blood and drank it. I will probably be dead by midnight whether they crucify me or not."

"What can we do to save you?" I asked.

Abigail hesitated and bit her lower lip with her even incisors, careful to keep her fangs concealed from us.

"Tell me what you need," I prompted.

She hesitantly replied, "I hate to say this, but I need blood, Eric."

"Not from any of us!" Josh growled through gritted teeth.

Douglas coughed and said in a strained voice that seemed to take his last reserves, "She can survive on squirrel blood or any animal."

"Right now I don't care," Josh said gruffly. "My town comes first and then we will worry about saving an undead."

"She is not an undead," I shot right back. "She is alive, just infected with the vampiric virus."

"Maybe so," Josh said, "but until we get this town squared away, we'll be of no help to anyone," He looked at Douglas and said, "We'll evacuate Douglas and the vampiress as soon as we can."

He turned back and stared at the guard and me, then said, "OK! Here is what we are going to do."

Edgy with pent up excitement and desire to do something, I stepped closer to hear and to obey his plans.

"Eric," he said.

"Yes, sir?" I replied, caught up with anticipation.

"I want you to--"

He stopped as a hinge creaked and a stream of light from above temporarily blinded us. I squinted as the door to the first floor fully opened letting the light seep in from up the staircase. I couldn't see the faces of the men silhouetted but I could clearly see their forms. Two men with M-16 tromped thunderously down the steps. Behind them was a tall athletically lean prisoner with his hands bound behind his back with a rope rather than handcuffs. Following the prisoner were two more guards with M-16s. Whoever the prisoner was, he scared them enough to issue four armed soldiers to guard the solo bound man. I strained to see his silhouetted face.

The two lead men pointed their guns at Josh and me and ordered, "You two! Turn around and place your hands on the wall."

I was surprised when Josh obeyed, so I followed his action of submission.

| 11 |

"Lieutenant Elmer Ranklin," Josh said, "It's me, Captain Josh Righter."

"I know damn well who you are. Now do as I said," Elmer commanded.

Josh complied. I could tell that Elmer was no pushover like the guard.

Their prisoner who they brought down the stairs chuckled grimly, "Eric! What the hell are you doing here? I should have known your dumbass would get captured."

The blindness from the upstairs light cleared up and I realized that their prisoner was Critter.

"I didn't get captured. I snuck in," I said with an odd bit of levity in my tone for the situation.

The tracker, whose eyes missed nothing, looked at my muddy boots, the tracks that led through the solid wall and nodded. "Sneaking into a dungeon. Not the brightest, eh? Most people try to sneak out, not in."

"You and I wound up in the same spot. Only you're tied up," I said.

"It looks like you got drafted, conscripted, and dressed in a uniform. You're more bound up and worse off than me."

I was confused for a moment until I remembered shaving and donning the black paramilitary uniform that Josh had given me.

Critter continued, "I just stopped in to see Craig and some friends for an amicable chat and these guys refused to return my gracious friendship."

"Shut up! You talk too damn much!" Elmer barked.

That cracked me up because Critter was one of the least talkative people I ever met. The usually quiet tracker tended to be the most talkative and smile the most when the odds were stacked impossibly against him such as now.

Josh took his hands off the wall and turned around to face the armed patrol. "You don't have Critter handcuffed. You tied him with a sloppy, knotted rope. Has protocol broken down so badly that you resort to such stupidity?"

Elmer said, "You should not have come back, Josh. You will face the death penalty when Craig finds out."

Josh stood his ground. His eyes were on the other men, but he spoke to Elmer, "You and this whole town will face execution if you keep following that drug-addled nitwit, Craig, and that Specter fiend that holds his leash. You fed me to his pet vampires, my friend."

Elmer raised his voice, "We let you escape. I've always respected you. I'll let you walk away today as well, but you must leave now."

"And I've always respected you as well, until now," Josh accused heavily.

"I have kids to feed," Elmer protested. "You aren't even married. You know what those Blackhawk helicopters can do. Within a minute, this town could be leveled and smoking with not a single inhabitant left alive."

"These freaks who you serve brought on the apocalypse. You'll raise your kids under their boots as if they were worms, like The Specter calls you. I do not fear death! I fear a groveling, despicable life! Grow some balls man! You should be getting Douglas some medical treatment, not letting your brother in arms die beneath your uncaring eyes."

"He tried to save that witch," Elmer said glaring at Abigail from the corners of his cold eyes.

Abigail sat silent, still too weak from her actions in the gymnasium to even offer her verbal defense. Sitting, looking over her bent knees that were raised up to her chin with her expressive eyes, she looked like an abandoned puppy in a kennel. A flash of anger and lust for The Specter's blood shot through my veins.

Seeing Abigail like this hit me hard. Just yesterday she was so full of life. I thought of the way she shot down the rope and landed next to me like a black descending angel after I fell through that trap door in the Caverns. I thought of her bright smile when I told a joke as we leaned on each other's backs. I thought of how we stood side by side when faced with an army of failed vampires with our flashing swords bright as her eyes. I wanted nothing more than to see that same life restored to the deep pools of her soulful eyes.

In the awkward pause, Douglas groaned and lifted his head up a few inches. His first words came out in a snuffling sound as blood formed a bubble and popped, spraying from his lips. "She saved me. She tried to save the others who The Specter fed to the vampires."

"She hypnotized you, you fool," Elmer accused. "They do that."

Critter said, "She also saved Bryan's kid and probably half our fighting men and women. She let us out of their caves when we were surrounded by an army of failed vampires. They had us dead to rights. It was only Abigail who saved us as she had a few other times before."

"I wouldn't be here without her either. I owe her my life," I said, "and I aim to repay that debt to her."

All eyes were on me. They wanted me to expound upon that statement. A flood of events hit me from the Vampire's Caverns to the time she appeared to us in the Mountain Warrior's ville to warn us of an invading army. When she walked into the tribe at that instant, the Mountain Warriors almost killed her in the mob like panic that the mere presence of a vampire could stir. It was only her sheer bravery that let her address us so that we realized that she was there to warn us. Overwhelmed with so many stories of her honor, I didn't know where to even start to defend her.

Critter spoke up, "Eric was down in their caverns alone with her for two days. She was ordered to kill him and didn't. That's one of the many reasons why they call for her execution. You fools can't see that she's a scapegoat for the real evil. Evil that you serve. She stands with us against it."

I nodded. This discussion in the dungeon cell was the closest thing to a fair trial that she could expect. I added, "She was ordered to turn me– To change me into a vampire or kill me. She had ample opportunity to do both but refused and helped me escape. You don't know what The Mind was, but she and I killed it. Because of that, the vampires, including her, have lost their psychic abilities. Look at her! She is helpless because of her own sacrifice to save humanity, you and your kids, Elmer!"

Douglas shifted as he jerked with surprise and painfully half sat up. He coughed and spat out some blood. He looked from me to Abigail. "You two killed The Mind?"

Abigail finally spoke up, "Yes."

"Holy cow!" he exclaimed before sinking back into the dirt covered concrete floor. His voice was strained with pain and weakness, but his eyes blazed with the duty to tell his tale as he lay flat on his back. He raised his head slightly again and said, "She did us a great favor. Y'all have no idea. He, The Mind, had some psychic control over us. He was a monster, about thirty feet tall. When I was taken to the Caverns, we were under some spell. We watched helplessly, as if in a stupor, as Sam was drained of his blood and then was fed to that thing called The Mind at the bottom of the pit. He died because of The

Specter's orders and Craig's complicity," Douglas explained. He had more to say, but It seemed that Douglas had used all his energy as he slumped back to the ground and closed his eyes. His face was wrenched in pain and he moaned lightly after a gurgling coughing fit.

Abigail looked at Elmer and explained, "It is why the vampires have lost a lot of their psionic control. It is why many of you have had increased desires to rebel against The Specter. It is why he is insistent on killing Douglas and myself. Because The Mind is dead, you can actually win this fight and free your town."

The men looked back and forth from each other and back at her. Some of them displayed a look on their face that I rarely saw in these wastelands: Hope.

She confirmed, "You began to desire your freedom more heartily just before sunset yesterday, didn't you?"

The men in the room looked around afraid to answer until they saw similar looks on each other's faces. Only then, did they nod.

With a grimace she stood up and shakily walked to the bars of her cell, facing everyone without fear. A determination lit her eyes as if her drive to defeat The Specter was all that fueled her movement. She gripped the bars with only enough strength to avoid collapsing. Reflexively, everyone except me stepped away from the imprisoned vampiress as she approached us from behind the solid bars.

"That's when Eric and I killed that monster. That's what freed your wills," she said. "The Nunnehi also turned off the vampires' access to," she hesitated as she looked for the correct word and settled on, "the Earth's powers. The Flow."

"Nunnehi?" Elmer exclaimed. Abigail had the full attention from everyone. The Nunnehi were a mythical faerie type of people from Cherokee legend. In the small towns of the region, everyone had heard stories of them as everyone in Ireland knows of the leprechauns. The difference is that the Nunnehi had not been reimagined through trite public holidays and silly gift cards.

"Enough with the faerie tales," Elmer said angrily with his head in the fight before him. "We have helicopters with hellfire missiles coming for us. No need for tall tales to scare the children."

"You mock superstitions and 'tall tales' of mythical creatures, as you argue with a vampire?" Abigail said with a weary smile on her lips, "In a town surrounded by a zombie horde, in a state ruled by a man named The Specter who wears a Halloween mask. And by your dumbfounded stares, I know that you felt the kernels of rebellion at the exact moment Eric and I killed The Mind."

"Enough." Josh raised his voice in a tone of the Commander of the Security Forces. "OK, here is what we are going to do."

I was impressed as the soldiers gathered around him. Josh had such a commanding presence that every eye rested on him with the desire to please their former Captain. Even Elmer lowered his gun to listen.

Josh continued, "Elmer, let them go from the cages. You two," he commanded, pointing at the two men who followed

Critter down the stairs, "go to the room with the infirmary supplies. There are stretchers in there. Get one. We're getting Douglas out of here and to a doctor. This is not how you treat a man who we have honorably served with. I would extend that same compassion for all of you men and you know it."

"Yes sir." The two men answered and left to fulfill their task to get a stretcher.

"And keep your mouth shut up there," Josh ordered the two soldiers.

Elmer looked with uncertainty at the two soldiers who had followed Josh's command and then realizing that he was outnumbered, Elmer immediately unlocked the cage that held Douglas. Josh walked inside and looked over the supine man quickly. I heard him ask questions about where things hurt and what type of pain. The other men stood over Josh waiting for orders.

I went to Abigail and touched her hand that grasped the bars. We rubbed each other's hands affectionately. I kept a poker face as I was startled at how icy cold her touch was.

"You look nice with a clean shave, or a beard for that matter," Abigail said with a brave smile.

"Thanks," I said, rubbing my face with my other hand, forgetting that I just shaved it, although my face felt every draft. I wanted to compliment her back. As I looked at her, I saw her beauty despite what they did to her, leaving her face pallid and devoid of life, but my mind was only focused on business, "I'm sorry about what I said last night. You were right about the blood madness that comes from the contact with vampire blood."

"I know. I dealt with that for nine months when they chased me."

"I know that you understand, but I wanted to apologize. I could tell that I hurt you." I neglected to mention how the mind meld thing she did freaked me out for fear that it would only make the others more suspicious of her when they heard of her power.

She replied with her dry humor, "I am fine. I am more miffed at The Specter at present. He does not suffer from blood madness and he sentenced me to death."

That brought me back to the urgency of our situation. "Hey, can we let her out as well?" I said, looking at Josh.

Most of the men looked at me like I was insane for letting a caged vampire loose. Josh looked at me and then to Elmer, "If Critter says she's OK and Douglas risked his hide like this for her, she's good people in my book, but I suggest you get the hell out of town with her immediately, Eric"

I sighed with relief and acknowledged his order. I really did worry that they would abandon her to the tortures of The Specter rather than free her. I was also happy that my adventures in this town that was on the brink of civil war were about to end. I did not want to get caught in the middle of a crossfire when the shooting started while carrying a blood drained vampiress incapable of walking on my shoulder.

Josh went back to checking over Douglas, but Elmer did not obey the order to set her free. He simply stared at the reestablished Captain of Security.

"Let her go!" I commanded Elmer, wanting to get the hell out of town.

Josh finally looked over his shoulder at Elmer, "What? Why are you just looking at me?"

"I can't let her go," Elmer said nervously.

"Why?" Josh straightened, like a venomous snake uncoiling as he stood up after squatting over Douglas. Josh demanded looking at Elmer with the intensity of a commander not used to being disobeyed.

"I can't release her," Elmer said.

"You can't or you won't?" Josh asked, as he stood to full height.

Elmer shrugged, "I can't. You see that chain around the door? Only The Specter has the key to that lock. Not even Craig."

I instinctively grasped the chain and gave it a violent yank. There was no way. The links were made of half inch steel and the lock was the size of my clenched fist. I knew it wouldn't give, when I yanked, but I was that desperate to free her. Despite my temptation, I also knew enough about ballistics to know that a bullet wouldn't break it, but rather ricochet until it hit someone in the stone room. I needed bolt cutters and big ones.

Just then, the men bounded down the stairs with the stretcher.

"Anyone with a shred of EMT training besides me?" Josh asked.

A few men raised their hands. They had quite a professional force, I knew.

"Good," said Josh. "Help me load him on the stretcher. Douglas, I think you're going to be fine, but we're going to move you as if we're concerned about spinal trauma as a precaution."

"Thanks, boss," Douglas muttered.

Before Josh bent to help load his soldier on the stretcher, he turned to Abigail and said, "And young lady? Don't you fret none. We're going to take care of Craig and get this town under control after kicking The Specter's ass out. While we're doing that, I'll send someone down here with bolt cutters to set you free. So don't you worry."

She weakly and silently nodded her reply.

Josh added, "The Specter should be back at nightfall. He is obeyed but only out of fear. I want to gather as many people as possible to our cause first and then launch our coup d'etat when he is here, so that the people of the town know that we are not fighting ourselves but rather the outsiders. I don't want to kill anyone from our town, but I have no problem putting a bullet through any brainpan of anyone that sides with that monster when they know the truth."

They loaded Douglas up with only a few groans from the battered man and gingerly carried him up the stairs. There was palpable excitement in the air. Despite their fear, they really desired to be free of The Specter's rule.

I looked at Abigail and said, "We will return for you."

"Eric," she said as I turned to leave, "take care of yourself."

The way she said it with finality in her inflection stopped me in my place at the foot of the stairs. I did a double take when I looked into her eyes. I can't describe it, but she looked as if she never expected to see me again. She knew that she was at the bottom of Josh's list of priorities. Even if Josh took back the town, a jailed vampire was still subject to mob justice that would reach fever pitch once The Specter was killed and she was in no condition to run, let alone even walk.

I walked back to the cage and looked her in the eyes and said, "I will return for you." When I grasped the bar she rubbed one of my fingers with hers. There was heated affection in the cold, bloodless touch, but her eyes still told me that she accepted her fate: that humanity had forsaken her.

It felt like my heart sank into my bladder as I rubbed her cold, blood drained hand with a caressing finger. Her hand felt like ice, literally. So much so, that I doubted her humanity if she could exist in her current state, but I knew what was in her heart was what made her who she was, even if she felt like a cold lifeless corpse at present. She was the most alive person I knew, and I owed her my life many times over.

"Abigail," was all that I could say at that moment.

"Eric! Move out!" Josh commanded from the stairs.

I nodded to her once more, "I will return for you. I swear," I repeated with a final rub on her icy hand. I then followed Captain Josh Righter's order. At the top of the stairs, I entered the hallway. Once the door was closed to the cellar, Josh grabbed me by the front collar of my coat and pinned me against the wall with a violent slam.

The captain glared into my eyes and demanded, "You are not falling in love with one of those vampires are you?"

"No! Of course not!" I said with fury as I pushed him away. Although I liked her, I still had a natural gut felt repulsion for anyone infected by that virus, but despite the gut reaction my heart was aflamed for her. I was just angry at the situation and directed it at him. A part of my anger was at myself for denying my affection for her. I then shoved his hands off of my collar as well.

"Good!" Josh said.

He turned to look at the men around him. A few soldiers who weren't part of the original group looked curiously at him as they entered the hallway. Josh waved them over.

They looked both surprised and happy as they greeted him with cries of "Captain Righter!"

He was greatly loved, respected, and feared by his men. That was a combination needed to effectively rule any group in these wastelands, especially when taking on the seemingly invincible powers that currently ruled. I had hope for what I thought was a hopeless situation.

Josh ordered the stretcher with Douglas to be taken to a van and told them to pick up Doc Cairns, and hide Douglas at the Ledford's hunting cabin.

He then ordered those gathered around that they all were taking over Craigsville.

"But the Blackhawks and Apaches?" Elmer stated.

All the men looked apprehensive. I even saw that fear flash across Josh's eyes.

Critter laughed lightly and leaned casually against the wall. All eyes now were on the usually silent tracker.

"What so funny, Critter?" Josh demanded as if the mocking laugh was a challenge to his tentative authority.

Critter nodded his head confidently upward. "What if I told you that I knew where to get a few dozen or so stinger anti-aircraft missiles up in these hills not far from here?"

Everyone looked at him in surprise.

I blurted, "The shoulder fired anti aircraft rockets?"

"No. Stinger pea shooters, Eric," Critter said with a deadpan expression.

Josh pushed me aside and got in Critter's face.

"How did you get them?"

Critter replied. "You know a country boy with some Cherokee blood in his veins has his ways. Give me a truck and I will have them for you before dark, but I go alone. I don't want anyone scoping my hideout."

Josh cocked his head and glowered at him, "Give you a truck? You won't just steal the truck like you did last time?"

"If I wanted to steal it, I would be gone already," Critter said.

"True," Josh agreed. "We'll get you the truck keys from Craig's office. Just don't wreck it like last time. These trucks belong to me now."

Critter nodded and said, "Let's go see Craig."

| 12 |

Josh led the way to Commander Craig's office. He tried the knob and saw that it was locked. He knocked.

"Go away!" Craig angrily commanded from the other side of the door.

Josh pistoned his leg and kicked the ancient oaken door open.

The men gaped at what they saw. Craig was sprawled on the floor, writhing in withdrawal pains. When he saw the men looking down upon his agony, the pain left his expression and pure rage at the violation contorted his face as he turned purple with the promise of delivering violence.

Then Craig sat up and reached for the goblet on his desk. As the tips of his fingers touched it, Josh knocked it away with a furious swipe of his hand. The golden droplets and goblet flew through the air and splattered against the wall as the cup clattered to the floor. Josh picked up the goblet as Craig stood on suddenly solid legs. In his eyes I could see that his strength was fueled by panic and need to feed his addiction.

Craig screamed, "You fool! You know not what you just did! You will die for this!"

"True. We all will die, but I am not in the mood to do so at right this moment." Josh said as he handed the goblet to a soldier behind him with the order. "Get this out of the room."

Josh then walked to Craig's desk and opened a drawer.

Craig started to protest and moved to stop Josh.

Critter stepped forward and slammed Craig against a wall, stopping him before the commander could interfere with Josh. Critter cocked his head and peered into Craig's eyes. The hard stare from the tracker silenced the commander as well as a Critter's knife under Craig's quivering jaw. Knives had an almost magical way of suddenly appearing in the tracker's hands.

Josh reached in the desk and pulled out a few packets that looked like the small envelopes that hold salt or pepper at fast food chains. There was no writing on them to give a hint of their contents. Josh clenched his fist around them.

Craig screamed as if the packets in Josh's vice-like grip were his heart. I realized that Josh held whatever drug that The Specter had him enslaved to. Two more men helped Critter hold Craig as Josh casually walked to the wood burning stove. Despite his earlier hell, Craig was suddenly propelled by enormous energy reserves. It was obvious that Josh held his life in his fist.

"No! No! Please! Please! No!" Craig cried in desperation. His anger was gone and replaced by pure pathetic desperation. "You don't know what you are doing."

Josh cast him a glance that said that he knew exactly what he was doing. When he opened the door on the woodburning stove and tossed them in, Craig grabbed his heart and fell to the floor sobbing helplessly, as he watched the fire spring to life, consuming the packets.

The soldiers stood silent. Usually men of this type would look down with disdain on such an emotional display that males are supposed to ditch in kindergarten. However Craig had always appeared larger than life in both physical mass and strength and mental prowess. The soldiers were overwhelmed by confusion as well as a terror of whatever had Commander Craig under such influence. If Craig could succumb to the unknown power, who could withstand it?

Craig quit screaming and his eyes widened with dread and he plopped to the floor with sudden weakness. "Please go." He begged Josh. "I don't want my men to see me like this."

"See you like what, my old friend?" Josh asked, but his eyes betrayed his knowledge of what was about to occur.

I could see a wave of pain overtake Craig. He grabbed his belly and writhed on the floor as he had been doing when we first entered the room. His hands moved all around his body as if trying to put out fires that only he could see and feel. In desperation he scrambled to his hands and knees and crawled as fast as he could to the wall where he immediately started licking the wet marks left by the drug laced wine like a feral dog licks a bone.

As his tongue met the wall, Josh backhanded and yelled with pure disgust, "Have some dignity man!"

"I will," Craig cried. "I just need a little and then I will be alright. I can see the sediment!"

Josh restrained Craig by his collar as if holding a pitbull back from attacking a mailman. The way Craigs eyes focused solely on the spots on the wall, I had a feeling that he was hallucinating and the unseen "sediment" appeared to him as the size of apples. Josh grunted and was about to hit Craig again.

"Here, here," said Critter with compassion as he walked to Craig and gently nudged Josh aside. He squatted at the boss of Craigsville's eye level and continued, "I used to work with addicts. I can help with your pain and addiction, Commander Craig."

Craig looked up to Critter, eyes wide with hope that pushed forth above the pain, "Really," Craig asked with almost wide eyed innocence.

"Yes," said Critter as he reached up to his own throat and removed his necklace from around his wiry neck. Craig watched with fascination as Critter slowly swung a silver cross before his eyes. "Look at the cross, my friend. Focus on its power and relax in your faith."

"Is this religious or hypnotism?" asked Craig as the cross had his full attention.

In a soothing, hypnotic voice, Critter said, "A little of both, my friend. Feel your eyes getting heavy as you look upon the gently swaying pendulum."

As Craig's eyelids started to droop, the necklace chain and the cross plummeted to the floor from Critter's suddenly lax fingers. As Craig's eyes widened questioningly, Critter's fist that had just held the chain smashed into Craig's temple. The big man went sprawling on the floor unconscious at Critter's feet.

Critter grabbed his necklace off the floor and stood back up with a bored look on his face. He casually leaned against the wall with his arms crossed before his chest, looking straight at Josh as he put the necklace back around his neck "We should probably take him to Doc Cairns' as well. He should lay up for a few days to get that poisonous garbage out of his system."

Josh chuckled grimly, "That was the right idea, Critter, but don't forget that this is my town. Ask me first before doing something like that."

Critter just shrugged. His stoney face betrayed no emotion or promise.

Josh wisely didn't wait for the woodsman to make any further indication of acknowledgement. Instead he turned to two of his other men.

"Act like Craig is any other recently deceased," Josh ordered. "Cover his face and load him into the A-Team on a stretcher with Douglas."

The "A-team" was what they affectionately called a souped up van that was just short of being a monster truck. It was painted black with garish flames on the side. With its spikes, armor, and gunports, I wasn't sure if they were totally serious or actually had a dark sense of humor about living in a post apocalypse world. Maybe it was both, but it ruled the streets that were stalked by zombies, vampires, and human bandits.

The men immediately obeyed Captain Josh Righter.

Josh tossed Critter a set of keys. "This is for that four wheel drive blue pickup. Do you need someone to go with you to load the Stingers?"

Critter caught the keys deftly and shook his head no, "I'd rather keep my sources secret. Give me a gate pass and I will be back in a few hours. I don't need to say it, but you have my word."

Josh smiled, "With your word, I don't even need a handshake. Thanks, brother."

Josh signed a blue card from Craig's desk and handed it over. Critter pocketed it, and they shook hands.

Usually the woodsman moved in a way that wasn't quite slow but rather deliberate and mindful. After pocketing the pass, he took off in a panther-like sprint toward the door. However, after casting a glance out the window, he stopped running.

"Hope you baked a cake," Critter drawled. "You're about to have company."

I looked out the window and saw about a hundred troops in formation marching to our position. They were less than a block away. They must have heard of Josh's return. The soldiers were ready for war. Their rifles were strapped to their backs and handguns holstered at their hips. Their fists gripped bats, swords, and machetes. A few carried bows and arrows. They would use quieter weapons since the zombies would follow gunshots for days after a discharge, instinctively knowing that something was dead or wounded and was an easy meal. Although easier to defend, the town at the back end of a valley acted like a natural channel for the undead, and there were reports of a large horde just a few miles away. This situation of wordlessly agreeing to silent combat reminded me of trying to fight quietly with my cousins as a kid to avoid attracting the attention of the adults. However, I wasn't sure how long that agreement would last. Everyone in the formation had firearms.

"Everybody out!" Josh ordered. "To the A-Team!"

We sprinted downstairs, through the hall, and to the front door. Josh stopped us before we exitted.

"OK," the Captain instructed, "Once outside, walk like we own the place. I want these men on our side. These are neighbors, not enemies. At least they aren't enemies until they attempt something stupid against us. We'll try talking first, got it?"

We nodded and Josh calmly led the way onto the porch like he indeed owned the place. The formation of soldiers marching toward us were between Critter and the blue pickup truck that he sought. The woodsman stopped walking and lazily leaned against an ancient tree with his hands open at chest level. He gave Josh a glance to see what would happen next.

The soldiers were fifty feet from us and about ten feet from Critter. There were enough of them to easily crush us. Our only options were to either win them over or escape in the A-Team van. Everyone was on edge. No one either side wanted to start a fight, but no one wanted to be first to take a sword slash or a bullet either

"Men!" Josh announced to the formation advancing toward us, arms akimbo. He stood ramrod straight, the portrait of authority. "I am Captain Righter, Head of Security! You know me. We have served loyally with each other. We are taking our town back from The Specter. You are still under my command. Company halt!"

The soldiers stopped marching, not as one but rather as a mob suddenly hit with confusion of their mutual purpose. I forced myself to breathe, to exhale, like the Mountain Warriors taught me. Everyone was on edge, and in the next second we could fall on either side of that deadly edge.

A man stepped forward and said, "Josh. Surrender. I am the new Captain of security since you were removed in disgrace. Put down your weapons and surrender."

Josh stood his ground and looked along the formation of soldiers. He confidently proclaimed. "I am still in charge and I order you all to join me. That includes you Johnathan," he added addressing the opposing commander.

The soldiers in the formation began to nervously discuss among themselves. I could see panic welling up in Johnathan's eyes knowing that his men were torn between which leader to follow.

"Attack!" Johnathan bellowed.

A tense second squeezed by and his men charged us. I saw Critter throw two knives simultaneously with his left and right hand. One stuck in Johnathan's chest. I didn't think it was a fatal wound as I watched him pull it out. His ribcage stopped it from penetrating deeper into his vitals. The other knife, thrown by his more accurate right hand, plunged in the soft vulnerable front of the throat of the soldier next to him. That man dropped instantly like a puppet with its strings suddenly cut with a sword stroke, but he was screaming as he clawed at the knife that still protruded from the bloody wound.

Critter pulled both of his swords from their scabbards and launched himself into the line. He flew right through them slashing through anyone in his way. He went from looking harmless into an instant screaming berserker and he burst through the confused line of men. Most of the soldiers rushed past him toward us as Critter raced to the pickup truck. I didn't see if he made it or not.

I stood there with my sword at the ready as they charged.

"Eric, let's go!" I heard Josh scream from behind me.

The captain leapt into the opening left by the sliding door of the van and the engine revved up with a rumbling roar. I raced to the van as I heard the soldiers screaming right behind me. The van peeled out as I dove through the door. I landed on top of Craig's unconscious body as Josh slammed the door shut behind me. The door grazed the heel of my boot. I heard some arrows pound against the steel door. I also heard a few gunshots fire and then pepper the van's metal, which meant that they really wanted us dead. I knew that they would pursue us relentlessly if they ditched the widely observed code of silence in battle.

As we sped away Josh swore savagely and punched the metal sides with enough force that I expected either his hand to break or the metal to dent, but both Josh and the A-Team van were an even match in resiliency.

I looked out the back that was more of a gunport than window and saw the soldiers rapidly left in our dust, still futilely chasing us on foot. Some went to one knee and fired at us. They were really serious.

We rounded a corner in a small, hilly neighborhood and could no longer see our foot pursuit.

The driver yelled back, "Cap'n. I radioed the gate. Charlie is working on it. He'll let us and Critter pass."

"He's a good man," said Josh.

I expected to see defeat on his face. However, I could almost see the gears of his mind smoothly running. In fact, his eyes seemed to be alive with life as if the mental grindstone of combat only sharpened his nerves.

We rounded a few corners, entering the outskirts of town in a rural, suburban mix, and Josh yelled, "Drop me off once you turn the corner by Miller's barn. Take Craig and Douglas to Doc Cairns. I am staying here to play. There are some folks who I want to talk to assuming Critter gets back with the Stinger Missiles."

"I want out too," I said.

"You'll slow me down, reporter," Josh said with annoyance.

"I'm not going with you," I stated.

He looked at me as if studying an insect and then smiled wryly. He swore and chuckled. "Watch it with her. I am sure she means well. She may be a decent person inside and pretty on the outside, but don't forget she is a failed government experiment. I am only telling you this 'cause I think you're alright, but horribly naive and in love with her. Watch it, OK."

"So I'm getting out with you?" I asked to make sure.

He ordered with a wry smile, "Sure, you may make a good distraction. Just go the opposite direction of me."

"I'm headed back to the mansion," I replied.

"I know, and that's fine. So am I. Just take a different route." he said with a grim smile as the van hit a pothole.

The van rounded a sharp curve behind a large red ancient but well cared for barn. The driver came to an abrupt stop but was careful to avoid squealing the tires.

Josh opened the side door. I jumped out behind him and I slammed it shut behind me as the van took off for the front gate.

"Take care, Captain," I said respectfully as I began to climb a fence to walk through a pasture back to the mansion.

"You too, mild mannered reporter," he said with a slight chuckle as he boldly walked on the road back the way we had just come from, toward the formation of soldiers who were out for his blood.

I shook my head and thought, *that guy has balls the size of North Carolina.*

| 13 |

I made my way back to the mansion within five minutes, but stopped a block away. I blended in with the gawkers. The place was surrounded by soldiers. Many licking their wounds with eyes alert and on fire for revenge. There was no way I could either force or BS my way into the headquarters building to rescue Abigail.

I saw Captain Johnathan holding a bloody bandage on his chest over his knife wound from Critter's throw. However, despite the injury, he was still very much in charge, and directing his people with barked commands.

I was actually somewhat surprised to see that the man who caught the knife in the throat was laying dead staring at the cloudy overcast with glazed eyes. Critter always said throwing knives were at best a distraction and not to be counted on as lethal weapons. Maybe that was a good rule for most people, but Critter was a wizard of death with knives. A pound of sharpened steel thrown at the neck was no joke, but it was worthless without the skill, power, and accuracy that Critter possessed in his lanky but powerful body..

I did notice that the blue pick-up was long gone, so I hoped that Critter was safe and long gone with it.

I turned to go down an alleyway and attempted to appear like I belonged in town. I was still wearing the black uniform of the security force so I made myself walk with the confident but grim swagger of a law enforcement officer doing his job ordained by human authority. No one questioned or bothered me as I walked past the mansion, careful to keep a distance of fifty meters or so from the group of soldiers. I told myself to act alert but calm. I did not want to answer anyone's questions or stand face to face with someone who would realize that I wasn't part of the town and certainly not the town's security force. I had to keep reminding myself that I was wearing their uniform.

I approached an alleyway when I heard a commanding voice behind me bark, "Soldier!"

I assumed it was directed at me. I was anticipating it and kept walking as if I didn't hear. I kept my shoulders loose, avoiding the temptation to bring them up protectively by my ears, betraying my anxiety at the sudden command.

"You!" the deep voice bellowed. "The one walking away!"

It sounded like he was only twenty five meters behind me.

I fought my instinct to break into a run, to walk fast, anything to get away. I hoped that my stride wasn't tripped up as I tried to be casual while deep inside, I felt my heart racing. My blood left my face flooding my legs with energy. The alleyway ahead was within five meters. A large stone building formed the corner. If I could just get around that and out of sight, I could run for it.

I casually cut across the grass of the yard on a worn trail to shorten the distance, fighting the urge to sprint.

"Stop! You! Stop right now! I know that you are hearing me!" I could hear his boots thundering on the pavement as the soldier issuing the orders started to walk quickly and urgently in my direction.

I now resisted the urge to turn around and look over my shoulder to put a face to the speaker.

"I order you to stop right now! I know you can hear me!"

I made it to the corner and slowly turned it. I heard the clomp of his walk turn into a run in my direction as he shouted, "Halt! Now! Or I will shoot!"

I rounded the corner and saw the alley was empty. As soon as I was sure that I was out of his sight, I started sprinting.

I heard the soldier order, "Get that man."

I could hear the pursuit in the numerous running boots over my own thundering boots. I sprinted twenty five yards and quickly ducked into another alley. After immediately turning a corner, I saw two dumpsters. I lifted the lid on the first one, but it was full of tons of junk. I almost didn't bother with the second, but I lifted it and it was half full of soaking wet, moldy sofa cushions. I threw some of them behind the dumpster, jumped in, and lowered the plastic lid as they rounded the corner. I cringed as the lid clacked loudly, but I could still hear the boots of the soldiers thundering past me.

I heard two sets of boots slow and stop inches away from me. My dumpster creaked as I heard someone touch it, probably leaning on it, I guessed from the pressure. I then heard a cigarette lighter and smelled the scent of tobacco and marijuana smoke.

"More fricken drama. I like Josh, but what the hell man?" said one soldier with a whiney voice. "Come on, don't bogart that!"

The other replied in a deeper voice but restrained as if holding the smoke in his lungs, "Here," he coughed and then said, "I, mean, I don't care. I am just trying to get out of this mess alive."

Then it was silent other than the occasional inhalations and coughs. I was really hoping that they would talk about something, give some information that I could use.

I dared not move. My breath demanded that I pant in ragged gasps from my short run and fiery adrenaline raging through my veins. I kept my breath quiet, but each stifled shallow breath seemed to starve me of oxygen even more. I was afraid that I would start panting like a playful Great Dane and give my position away to the smokers of the spliff.

Their conversation started up again, but it was mostly about the drudgery of military life. I could tell both were leaning against the dumpster face to face. I was tempted to surprise them, pop open the lid, and knife them. That probably wouldn't work, but I felt desperate as I waited in the darkness of the smelly hideout.

My breath finally stabilized. Their conversation turned towards women, sports, and cars. My uncle always said you could tell a dumbass, because those three topics were the only subjects of conversation that they could discuss. The only thing missing from the conversation was booze and partying, but they were already smoking a spliff on the job.

I sniffed my surroundings as I was afraid being in a dumpster would leave me smelling like moldy, rotted crap the rest of the day and attract suspicion as I moved among the townsfolk to free Abigail, but I didn't smell much rot. The trash had not been collected in two years. The stench of garbage was gone. There was only a smell of mold from the wet cushions that had probably been in here for two years. My butt and right leg were damp where I contacted another wet mattress, but I was sure that wetness would dry with a half hour of walking and hopefully with post-apocalypse hygiene, no one would notice the musty smell.

"You two! What are you doing?" a third commanding voice barked from a few meters away from us. It sounded like the soldier who originally barked at me to stop. The one who had initiated the pursuit.

The dumpster groaned as the two men removed their weight to stand up straight.

"Nothing sir."

"I see that. I told you to pursue whoever that was."

"We thought we heard a noise in one of these dumpsters and investigated."

"And have a 'cigarette?'" the leader said with disdain. "Did you see anything in the dumpster?"

"No sir. Just trash."

"Are they ever going to start collecting trash again, sir?"

"Get back to earning your pay and give me that smoke," the commander ordered.

I jumped with a startle and then cringed as a fist slammed solidly onto the lid. The impact reverberated through my bones.

"Yes sir!" the two men said. I pictured them saluting in the position of attention as their voices sounded strained. I then heard the boots retreating at a lazy jog.

I then heard someone taking a drag off the spliff. I guessed it was the soldier who had initiated the chase after me.

I gripped my handgun and ducked deeper as the lid was opened. The lit hand rolled cigarette butt landed in my hair. I resisted the urge to swipe it away. The lid slammed and I could smell my burnt hair. I then smacked the burning butt away, smelling the cloying scent of burnt hair and spliff as the clomping boots of the commander retreated into the distance.

After a few minutes of silence, I slowly lifted the lid with just enough space to check the alleyway. Twenty meters away, I saw Elmer and a few other soldiers sharing a cigarette and looking at the not so distant mountains as they discussed the events. I slowly lowered the lid. A few seconds later the lid lifted and another butt flew into the dumpster. This time it landed away from me and the lid slammed shut again.

I willed my muscles to relax and waited about a quarter of an hour. I actually counted the seconds to both ensure that plenty of time passed and to calm my nerves.

I peeked out again. With the lid open a crack, I carefully scanned the alleyway. The coast was clear. After another minute, I closed the lid as I heard boot stomps. A large group of soldiers approach. They were relaxed and carrying on a conversation. I distinctly heard one guy say, "Whoever that was is long gone."

In the distance, I heard Elmer bark, "Every swinging dick, get back to headquarters, on the double."

I heard a few whines of complaint and then the walking clomp of the boots hastened into a lazy jog.

I guessed that Elmer and Jonathan were now in firm opposition to Josh Righter.

I waited another minute and slipped out of the dumpster.

I walked back to the dilapidated barn with the hopes of getting back into the dungeon through the tunnel. I used the relatively towering school buildings as a reference. I worried about wandering through a town that I wasn't familiar with, while being pursued by soldiers who probably knew every alley, dumpster, house, and person who lived here, but the streets were relatively clear in this area.

Despite the tunnel seeming to go on for an eternity, following the alleys, it took me less than a minute to get to the barn.

Once inside the barn, I stood over the hidden opening. I didn't want to go back through there, and I felt like I was taking that moment most people do while considering the stupidity before doing a high cliff dive into a small pool in a creek. I bent to remove the heavy grate.

However, I stopped suddenly. I forgot to get bolt cutters. I swore under my breath and stood there for a moment. I then went to the front end of the barn and came to a locked door. I looked at the ancient lock and easily raked it open with my modified paper clip and tension wrench.

Inside the small room, I didn't see anything of value with a cursory look over. On the counter, I saw just rusted hammers, screwdrivers, and pliers. I opened a few drawers and slammed them shut when I saw only washers, screws and bolts of all sizes. I cringed at the noise that my angry, frustrated movements made.

I took a deep breath and blew it out and looked at a small closet. The door was constructed of white painted boards with ragged quarter inch gaps between them. I opened the creaky hinges and sighed in relief as I squinted in the dim light but instantly tensed in surprise.

Hanging from a hook was a new, well oiled set of bolt cutters with handles that looked two and a half feet long. They looked sharp enough and long enough to get the leverage to cut through that chain around Abigail's cage door. I tensed because nothing in the Forbidden Zone was ever that damned easy.

I picked it up, studied, and worked with the mechanism. I didn't want to make more than one trip through that dank passage with a weak flashlight. When I was satisfied that it would probably work, I turned around and went back to the trapdoor to the tunnel.

As I stood hesitating above the trap door, I heard the thump of The Specter's helicopter landing in the direction of the mansion. I had no time to waste.

I turned on my headlamp and entered the dark world below. Once I got my bearings, I turned off my headlamp and walked blindly in the darkness. The story of my life, I mused without regret.

This time I didn't mind stepping into the ankle deep water because my feet were already miserable in the soaking wet socks and boots. I marched quickly with one arm feeling the way, in front of me and occasionally touching the wall beside me.

Halfway through the tunnel, I felt that there was a smaller side tunnel with my hand. I hadn't noticed it the first time because I saved the hard to get batteries of my lamp and relied on Josh's. I stopped, flicked on the light and studied the side passage for a moment. I checked my compass that was on my lapel and saw that It headed north, into the direction of the mountain behind the town. I shuddered as I looked through the thick cobwebs that I would have to run through if I tried this way. I will repeat it: I hate spiders, maybe as much or more than vampires. It looked like I would have to stoop to go in there through an old rocky tunnel barely five feet high. I wondered if it was a possible escape route with Abigail to the wild safety of the mountains. I couldn't see trying to walk with a vampire through this town.

I turned off the light and ran through the muddy water, suddenly hit with a sense of urgency. I reached the solid wall and felt around for the secret place to push. I pulled the handgun out of my appendix holster and let it lead the way in place of my flashlight. I wasn't sure who I might face in the dungeon, but as outnumbered as I was in enemy territory, I wasn't going to play by the usual unwritten law of no shooting. With the pistol in my hand, I pushed open the hidden doorway and entered the dungeon, ready for war.

| 14 |

Abigail lay alone in a heap with her head propped up on the stone wall of the dungeon. It was hard to just breathe. She had hardly any blood left to transport the oxygen that she inhaled. She caught her breath and coughed weakly as she heard the door open, hoping against hope that it was a rescuer. She had doubts after hearing the earlier gunfire outside of the building.

But her hopes were dashed as she heard the stomp of boots on the stairs and saw the flowing cloaks of the vampires with The Specter.

They weren't taking chances. There were twenty of them in all, counting the vampires and soldiers.

The Specter's inhumanly deep voice boomed a command, "Stand up, Abigail. It's time."

Her muscles contracted but she couldn't obey as he unlocked her cell door, but it didn't matter. She wanted to stand on her own, but now she was frozen. It was the realization that her fate was sealed that shut down any power she had over her already weakened muscles. She was used to surviving on her own and they had taken that ability away with her blood. Her only friend was Eric, but for him to make a rescue attempt would be as pointless as one man attacking a state penitentiary. The only difference was that instead of Eric facing a trial for making a rescue attempt from a state prison, he would immediately join her on a cross. It would be wise if he just ran. In fact she hoped for his sake that would be what he was doing now.

Her coven, including Dexter, rushed inside the cell as the human soldiers stood back in fear of the bloodless, motionless vampire. She kept her eyes closed knowing that the blood madness in her eyes would further horrify them. Half the time her eyes were like the dying wick of a candle. Occasionally, the vampiric need would fire them up with raging desire. Now they were raging

The Specter rumbled to the human guards, "This is the vampire who has been preying on your families and friends."

Dexter lifted Abigail's head up by her hair and placed a large iron ring around her neck. He spoke nothing but his smug grin said everything.

The other vampires attached four, six feet long iron bars on the ring. Then they yanked her to her feet.

The Specter then assured the human guards, "With those bars, she will be unable to inflict a bite on any of you, but use caution. She's deadly."

She collapsed but was then lifted to her feet again and pulled out of the cell by the bars attached to the steel ring around her neck.

"Don't be fooled by her fake passiveness," The Specter warned again. "Hold the bars tight."

Two guards grabbed the front bars and two grabbed the bars behind her. She realized that the bars weren't there to protect the people but rather to carry her in her helpless condition. They led her up the stairs and out to the place where she was to be publicly crucified. All of her hope was gone as she could only struggle to breathe against the iron ring around her throat.

***

With my handgun leading the way, I entered the chamber of the dungeon. My heart instantly sank. The vampiress was gone. The cell doors were left wide open. There was no one in the empty dungeon other than myself. Even the guard had left. I could hear many steps and voices on the floor above me. I guessed they were upstairs and waiting for nightfall to lead her to her public execution.

I cursed silently and tiptoed up the stairs, cringing with each slight creak of the ancient wood. I listened at the wooden door and could hear the tromp of soldiers' boots in the hallway above the dungeon and the rough, uncut deep voices of the soldiers' boisterous talk.

I tried to listen for any information that might tell me where they took her or anything else that might be of value to know. I heard them express sympathy for Josh in hushed tones, then I heard louder talk punctuated by laughter as they conversed about booze, women's anatomy, and motorcycles, surprisingly all at once.

I sighed and tip-toed back down the stairs, entered, and closed the secret door to the dank tunnels. I couldn't rescue her in this building. If I was to save her, it most likely would have to be during her execution, in front of the crowds of hundreds of jeering agitators and armed soldiers. Where I would likely be crucified beside her or if I was lucky, beat up until I could do nothing but belch blood bubbles like Douglas. That's if I attempted a rescue. It seemed hopeless at this point. I thought this as I trudged through the water, more sloshing than splashing as my feet dragged in the mud as if weighted with boots of lead.

It would be a nearly impossible task to rescue the vampiress. No one would blame me for backing out. It would be suicide to attempt anything. I wanted to run back to the camp of the Mountain Warriors and pretend that I never entered Craigsville, but Critter would know that I had been here.

Critter, I reminded myself with a sliver of hope. He should have the anti-aircraft missiles, but what could he do? Not much more than me. Whether people were for or against Josh, it didn't matter. The town was united against the vampires, particularly Abigail at this moment.

I was determined to leave the town without attempting a rescue. There was nothing that I could do against a town of one thousand people set on killing her, and me, if I attempted to rescue her. It was beyond the power of one lone man. A journalist, who barely two weeks ago sneaked through the barbed wire fence unarmed to get in here.

I climbed out of the tunnels and into the barn. I slid the grate over the hole and sat on the dirt floor of the barn with my head buried in my hands. I wasn't sure what to do, run or fight. Again I told myself that no one would hold it against me if I ran from such overwhelming odds. If I was going to fight and rescue her, I had a lot to think about, a lot to do and judging by the receding daylight, I had less than a half hour to do it, but I had no energy to do anything. No energy to attempt to save her. It was suicide, I kept thinking as I sat on my ass in the dark barn with my head buried in my hands. I could only do it if Josh returned with an army, but he seemed to be patient, and willing to wait until his time to strike was right. I had no one I could rely on. Which meant that Abigail had no one that she could rely on. My only hope was to deliver a clean head shot to end her misery.

I tried to tell myself that Abigail knew that I couldn't do anything. She seemed to have understood that as we shared our last look in her cell. The heartbreak and desire to do what was right waged a war with my fear and survival instinct and fear was the clear victor in that collision, but that war plunged me into a depressive state where I was incapable of taking any action.

"Abigail…" I said telepathically. I didn't think it would get to her with everything shut down.

I faintly heard her say in my mind, "Eric. Run! I am through--"

And then there was no connection. Was it all my imagination? Madness?

Bryan had once told me that as a leader, you may not know what to do, but freezing was the last thing that you wanted. He said when stuck in a tight situation, do something, anything and make the plan as opportunities arise.

I dwelled on the thought that no one would blame me for backing out of a rescue attempt, but I knew that that wasn't true. I would blame myself and carry it to my grave. Everything that led to this moment was my fault whether from Abigail giving her life to save me or through my own stupidity and madness, I had abandoned her at the caverns. I had scorned her in my madness earlier when I should have escaped with her. I owed her my life.

I bolted to my feet. I would do something. What? I had no clue. I put on my coat so no one would suspect me of impersonating the security force, and I left the barn with the intent to do something, anything.

| 15 |

It was thirty minutes to sunset as I walked past the gymnasium where the kangaroo "trial" was held. I was thinking that might be where the execution was to take place. I rushed there quickly, but no one was in sight.

Although the town was small and I had been here briefly in the past, I still found myself somewhat lost. A brisk winter wind cut through my hair and stung my now beardless face. A cold that felt like a sharp burn, but then caused my bones to shudder. I threw up the hood, not just for warmth, but also a slight disguise. There weren't many people on the street, but everybody did know everybody at least at a glance. It would be best to maintain whatever anonymity that I could manage.

I rounded a corner and recognized the old white boarded up pharmacy. I kept my head down as I walked past it because I had talked to the pharmacist on the last visit and wasn't sure where he stood on the issue of Josh and the vampiress. I forgot his name, but I knew that he was an old Vietnam Veteran. He moved stiffly with age, but his eyes held a fire that told me he was capable of drawing from that youthful well of a warrior in powerful spurts.

As I passed by the old building, I pushed any thought of the old man away from my mind.

"Hildebrande," called a gravelly voice from behind me.

I didn't even flinch as I pretended that I did hear anything.

"I know that is you and that you heard me, Eric Hildebrande," he said in a quieter voice so as not to give me away.

I took a few more steps keeping my shoulders relaxed as my brain processed how to proceed, but I couldn't pretend that I didn't hear the old man.

I finally stopped and turned. I lifted my head and looked at him.

"Come on into the store, son. You'll freeze to death outside," he said as he turned his back to me and stiffly walked up the few stairs. He held the door, letting the precious heat flow outside as he waited for me to join him.

"You're a bit of a mess, son," he said as he looked over the cobwebs on my coat and mud on my soaked through boots and lower pants legs. "Have a seat," he said as he threw a wrist-sized stick into his small wood burning stove that had burned down to faintly glowing coals. A kettle of simmering water sat on the stove giving a pleasantly warm humid atmosphere.

I looked over the shelves and saw a mix of prescriptions in the bottles of the manufacturers, mason jars full of home concoctions, and some of his weaponry. He was quite a collector. He had everything from ancient Mongolian horse bows to modern rifles.

I declined his offer to sit as I replied tersely, "No. I'm a bit busy right now. Hell, I'm not sure why I even came inside with you."

"Young'uns, always in a hurry these days." He said, taking on a mock shaky voice to sound even older. It was as if he didn't realize that he was an old man with an already gravelly voice. He added with a smile, "If one studies history, you should take your time when entering into a revolution, but that is a young man's game. For the rash who do not have a family to worry about." He motioned to a chair with the finality of an old man who is not afraid to make demands of others.

I sat. These were a couple of padded worn out chairs, where equally worn out old men sat to talk.

"You take the side of The Specter?" I asked.

"Oh, hell no. I'll go down in a hail of bullets for Josh, if my death would mean anything, but I don't think it would. People love him, but they fear the wrath of The Specter and his death birds even more and for good reason. I saw their power in 'Nam and the choppers are exponentially worse these days. Even more horrible, they aren't on our side in this war."

"Critter may bring back some shoulder fired anti aircraft missiles." I replied, worrying that I said too much, immediately after the words left my mouth.

His eyes lit up with the excitement of a young warrior as he said, "Good. Are you hoping to help Josh on this fool's crusade?" he asked

"Yes, but I have an even more foolish crusade. I'm planning to rescue the vampiress," I said, looking straight into his eyes for his reaction. I purposely went for the shock value. I wanted everything on the table to see how he would respond. The best thing he could do was talk some sense into me, I thought. If the worst happened, I was well aware that my weapons were within easy reach as were his.

His eyes widened only slightly for the briefest moment. Then he laughed ruefully. "I'm guessing she may almost be worth it. Douglas Bircher is a solid young man and probably gave his life for her earlier today. I hope he's alright. My grandson played football with him. Just don't end up like poor Douglas, if the vampiress is going to die anyway." He ended with a regretful shake of his head.

"Josh rescued Douglas from the dungeon and is getting him some medical care," I said. I knew that I should be keeping my mouth shut, but I hadn't been able to talk to someone about all this in quite some time. It actually was helping to quell some of the fire raging in my mind as well as the debilitating depression to talk to someone who I respected and despite not knowing him well, I instinctively trusted him.

The old man added, "Douglas was, or is, a good man but too easily swayed by his passions, like you."

"I'll try to come up with a better plan. I think Josh is going to do something around sunset. That's when I plan to act."

"That's a little wiser," he said as he picked up a long ancient rifle with a scope from his wall display. The modern optics looked out of place on the dark brown with lighter colored chips in the stained wooden stock and handguard. I recognized it as an old Russian made Mosin Nagant sniper rifle. There were a few of them floating around that I had come across. Kristy, the best sniper in the Mountain Warriors tribe could shoot a flea off a dog's ass at two thousand yards, according to Scott. Or maybe he said that she could shoot a flea's ass off of a dog's back. Knowing him, he probably had said both at different times, depending upon his sobriety.

The old man continued on as if I had all the time in the world to sit and listen to him talk with an old man's wistfulness, "I am too old to join in running battles, but with a scope and steady hands, this old timer can give support from a good distance. Depending upon how things go down, I may be able to give you the slightest edge."

I thought of suggesting that he give Abigail a clean headshot, but instead, I stood back up with determination and said, "I need to go."

He laughed.

"What?" I angrily snapped, not feeling like being mocked as my mind was in turmoil. Nevermind whether I deserved his laugh or not.

"Do you even know where you are going?" he asked.

"No," I sighed and sat back down in a flopping heap. I was infamous for my impulsive and rash actions. Here I was jumping up and ready to head off somewhere with no direction as usual.

"Where will they try to execute her?" I demanded.

He opened his mouth like he was going to remark about me claiming that they would "try" to execute her. He sighed and said, "At the football field," he answered. He pointed to a tourist map on the wall, where the buildings were drawn as caricatures, but I recognised some of the landmarks of the town and I now knew where I was heading.

"Then that's where I'm going," I said, standing up from the chair again.

He shook his head no and said, "Ambushing on the way there might be a better idea. They should be leaving the headquarters building soon. They aren't going to parade the vampires before the sun has set, even as dismal as the winter sun is on this cloudy day."

"Maybe so," I said and started to walk to the door, but I was startled as I heard a buzzing noise that was both nostalgically familiar and jarringly rare. A cell phone, I thought. It had been a while since I heard one. The last time was in Dexter's fortress.

"Excuse me," he said.

I watched in surprise as he picked up a cell phone.

"You have a cellphone?" I asked incredulously..

He held off answering the phone as he told me, "I'm one of the few with a phone. As a pharmacist, I'm one of the few acting 'physicians' in the town." He pressed a button and answered the phone. "Hello."

His old face wrinkled up even more with perplexity as he looked up from the phone and toward me. "It's for you."

I gritted my teeth knowing damn well who it was. A drone must have spotted me. I grabbed the phone from him.

"What the hell do you want, Tommy!" I exclaimed.

"I don't have much time, but your uncle has been deposed. You don't have the protection–"

"Protection!" I snarled spitefully. It should have hit me harder that my uncle was deposed, but the desire to save Abigail as well as the craving to beat the shit out of my former friend who betrayed me multiple times raged in my mind.

"Listen, Eric."

"No you listen, you son of a bitch!" I shouted. I gripped the phone in an iron fist. I was almost surprised that it didn't shatter from the force of my hand. "An innocent woman is about to be killed."

"The vampiress?" Tommy asked with the judgemental voice of a jury delivering a sentence of capital punishment.

"She saved my life! She saved the lives of the few friends that I have."

"Eric!" Tommy persisted. "They're doing you a favor by killing her. She will turn you or worse. She has you under her psychic powers. You're throwing your life away. She is a vampire. She is literally death!"

"No she isn't!" I suddenly found myself near the point of an emotional breakdown. I was afraid that I would tear up for a moment. Instead, I raged. "You stole my girlfriend Jennifer! You had me exiled into the Forbidden Zone. You've ruined me in every way possible. Now you people are going to kill Abigail!"

"Eric, listen–."

I turned my back to the old pharmacist. I feared that I would break down crying in front of the tough old man as I turned on Tommy. "She is the only good person I know. You're trying to kill the only person who matters to me!"

"Eric. That's insane."

I raged on as my pent up feelings were finally released, "Why man? Why? What did I ever do to you? You can't kill the only person in the world who I love."

"Love?" Tommy wisely kept his usual mocking tone out of his voice. He spoke both sternly and reasonably. "She's a bloodsucker. The Specter's doing you a favor, bro."

I was speechless and could only scream curses at him. Before my heated tears of fury could spill, I yelled, "Either save her or stay the hell out of my way, asshole."

"You should thank us for killing her."

I almost threw the phone in anger, but instead, I shouted, "Stay the hell out of my life, you son of a bitch."

I attempted to hang up as Tommy was trying to explain something in an infuriatingly reasonable tone. Instead, I tried to turn off the phone so that he couldn't immediately call back, but I was out of sorts and my trembling hands could only fumble the device as I punched the screen with my finger a few times, but it didn't hang up. I finally handed the phone back to the pharmacist before I could destroy it in a tantrum.

"Sorry," I told the pharmacist for my ranting and almost destroying his phone.

He just nodded and said, "I can see she matters a lot to you."

The phone line was still active and I could barely hear Tommy calling my name as the old man calmly pressed the screen and cut off the call.

"Yes she does," I said. That outburst encouraged me. I had kept those feelings bottled up. After saying out loud that I loved her, I could not deny my feelings for her.

My gaze shot at him as the phone rang again. The pharmacist looked at the phone and then scowled as he looked at me.

"Same number," he said.

I knew that I should talk to Tommy because he could at least fill me in on some questions. Even if he lied, which I knew he would, I could at least get a sense of what he was scheming based on what he was trying to talk me into doing or not doing. Instead, I shook my head, "No. I'll probably destroy your phone if I hear that son of a bitch's voice again."

He nodded and drawled in another exaggerated mocking tone of an old man, "Now we can't have you doing that now, can we sonny boy?"

"No we can't. I gotta go," despite the situation I expressed a quick wry half grin at the exaggerated old man's voice that he did.

"Well go, but go with God," he said with a salute that tapped his forehead.

I nodded without looking at him and left.

Sunset was a quarter hour away. I hoped that if the choppers showed up, Critter would be back with the rocket. If those flying gunships showed up without Critter's rockets, this would be one of the shortest lived, attempted coup d'etat in history, if one was even attempted.

***

After escaping from the headquarters building, Critter drove to the gate. He handed the blue gate pass signed by Josh to the gate guard as he said with lazy good naturedness, "Good to see you again, Bill, especially without you shooting at me." He kept a smile to himself as he looked over the hasty repairs that they applied to the gate after he, Bryan, and Eric slammed through it barely a week ago with the Humvee that they had stolen from Craig on their last escape. The destruction he made of the gate gave him a sense of pride as an artist would take in looking at his completed sculpture.

The guard, who was an old friend of Critter's, laughed back, "Hey, you were stealing the boss' ride man. Nothing personal."

"I respect that you were doing your job," Critter said.

"And I respect that you were doing yours. I'm glad I missed your skinny ass, but I suggest you go quickly. I don't know how long until they revoke Josh's order. I'm just a peon, after all."

"Yeah, I'd like to chat–" The usually quiet Critter replied with his lazily wry smile.

"You never chat. Hell, you barely ever say a word. That's what I like about you. Everyone else constantly tells me that I am full of shit. You just nod at what I have to say."

"Well, you are full of it, but I figured that you already knew. Now open the gate, my friend."

"You got it," Bill said as he left to help the other guards lift the heavy bolt and started to open the gate for Critter. As he put the truck in drive, Critter heard the shouting of soldiers as a few were running toward them too close for Critter's comfort, "Detain that man!" one shouted. "Don't let him pass through that gate!"

Critter slammed the gas and plowed through the gate, slamming through the small opening. He ducked down as he saw in the rear view mirror a few soldiers aiming their rifles but none fired as he sped away. He was already through, but he was sure a convoy of armed men would shortly be in pursuit. The tracker kept the pedal floored.

He grimly chuckled to himself as he passed the wreck that they made of Craig's hummer in the woods just off the road. Craig never bothered to recover it. They had wrecked it that badly. In the post-apocalypse world with no factories making spare parts, salvaging was all they had. It seemed they didn't want to waste the effort in recovery at this time.

Critter, the man of few words, had peed on the interior as a parting shot. My art is destruction. The tyrannical world is my canvas, Critter thought as he smiled to himself.

As he drove, he was tempted to simply drive off and keep the stolen pickup truck. It wasn't that he didn't keep his word, but the temptation of bringing a truck back to his tribe would benefit his friends so much that the temptation strongly pulled at his mind. Also, the rockets weren't his to give away but rather his crazy brother's.

However, the good people of the town were counting on him. Josh and a few others were friends from childhood and although he didn't know Eric that long, he had come to respect him. Rarely had he seen such determination in anyone. If Eric could keep his head, Critter was sure he'd be a warlord someday in the Forbidden Zone.

Besides, the idea of shooting down some of The Specter's warbirds appealed to his sense of justice, but still, deep inside a part of him would rather steal the truck than his brother's rockets. Grand theft auto was really the wise thing to do, "But I feel foolish today," Critter said out loud. In the quiet interior of the truck with only static on the radio, Critter found himself talking to himself on the drive.

The thirty minute drive passed quickly. He hadn't driven on these roads since it all went to hell two years ago. A few zombies staggered after his wake but nothing horrible happened. However, he kept his gun beside him, safety off, bullet in the chamber, and ready.

What got to him the most and settled in his stomach was the weight of regret that felt like fifty pounds of lead in his gut. The regret was knowing that the empty buildings of homes and businesses that had been owned by friends who were probably dead. He was reminded of the destruction wrought upon the world. The busted windows from looters such as himself (although he and his tribe attempted to be less destructive) and the disrepair was bad enough, but knowing his friends who had owned and rented these buildings were dead or worse, zombies, felt like a fist into his solar plexus that hit with that lead weight of regret. If they did survive, it was only in Craigsville, under the tyranny of The Specter.

"Yeah, I'm fulfilling this mission," Critter grimly said as he made up his mind not to steal the truck, for now. Maybe he would after bringing back the rockets. Maybe. Despite the seriousness, stealing the truck felt like a game to be played with his old friends from boyhood.

He turned off the paved road onto a decent gravel road, and after a mile, he made a turn onto a dirt road that was more of a fire trail. It was so eroded that he was sure that the rockets were most likely untouched. The road, which was barely a path, went up some steep inclines. Even on the quick, bumpy ride, his sharp eyes could see that there were no tire or boot threads in the clay of the exposed road. No one had been up this way in some time.

He arrived at his family's hunting cabin and avoided looking around the place in fear that the emotions of a lost past would tug at his heart. There were lots of good times here with family and friends, good times full of beer and cheer, that were long gone. Instead, his eyes shot to wherever an enemy could be hiding.

He scowled when he saw that the door of the cabin had been kicked down. Gun in hand and itching for a fight at seeing the violation, he rushed in the cabin, fearful that his brother's rockets had already been stolen. Indeed, the trap door that had been covered by a rug was open. He descended the stairs and saw that everything had been looted. His brother's stash of MREs were almost all gone. The plastic crates that held the launchers were opened.

However, he laughed as he looked in the crates. The launchers and the rockets were still there. Obviously, the looters saw no use for them. If you shot a deer with them, there would be no meat left and lugging them out of the cabin would have been a waste of energy that no one had these days. Not to mention, most people wouldn't know how to fire one safely even for the entertainment of pyrotechnics.

"Sorry brother," he muttered as he picked up a rocket to load the truck with his brother's weaponry.

His brother was far worse of a survival nut than Critter himself. The fiery combination of redneck and Cherokee blood in his veins held no trust in the current world system. Even Critter had thought that his brother had been overreacting with rockets. Now he saw his brother as a prophet.

A part of him felt more guilty about stealing from his brother than his thoughts of stealing the truck, but the rockets would be put to good use. His brother, who was somewhere in Florida, couldn't access them and would approve of what he was going to use them for anyway.

Critter loaded up five rockets into the truck bed and left twelve more behind. He then closed the trap door and covered it with the rug.

There were only a few MREs left. He sat down and ate one, taking his time. He wanted to get back to Craigsville around sunset. If he showed up too early when it was still daylight, he was concerned that one of Craigsville's security patrols would spot him.

It was odd. He was seemingly a wild man at heart and preferred fresh cooked venison to anything prepackaged, but he found himself savoring the pineapple cake in one of the MREs. It resembled a stale Poptart that had been rendered to dust in a blender and then mashed and reassembled together. It wasn't the most tasty dessert, but it tasted like life before the constant fear of the present. It tasted like good times. Artificial and fleetingly fragile, but nostalgic nonetheless.

Finally as the sun began to peek under the trees on a nearby mountain that towered far above him, he climbed behind the wheel. He looked at the sun hovering over the western horizon one last time. Only a few scattered rays escape the gray clouds. With the melancholy he felt in this place, he had spent more time here than he had intended. He would get back to Craigsville after sunset. He hoped that it wouldn't be too late for the fun.

| 16 |

With finding the pharmacy and getting advice from the old veteran as well as looking at the tourist map, I had a better idea about where I was and the layout of the town, but I still had no plan, only a sense of wild urgency. With my winter hood up, I walked in the direction of the mansion that was on the way to the field. A cold wind still cut deep through my layers and seemed to reach my heart.

I avoided taking a direct route, but a more circuitous route to observe. I was a block away from headquarters when my heart sank. A procession of soldiers and civilians lined the streets. I was outnumbered hundreds to my one. Or more like one thousand to one. No one would fault me for backing out of a rescue attempt but me, I knew.

On the streets, the crowd parted as armed men, with guns displayed rather than their swords, pushed and prodded

Abigail. Abigail was thirty meters away and headed in my direction. The soldiers weren't playing with a convicted vampire. A steel ring was locked around her neck. Four, six foot long iron bars held by four different soldiers prevented her from attacking anyone, but it looked like the restraint was more to hold her upright and push her along.

However, I could see this precaution was unnecessary simply by looking at her face.

I wasn't sure what exactly she meant when she said that they had drained her blood. However in the waning daylight of this cloudy twilight, the paleness of her face was horrifying. She looked even worse than earlier. For me, the paleness showed her pain and her near death exhaustion. To the crowd around her, she looked beyond death already. Monstrous and undead was the best description to describe how she looked to the death jeering mob.

I heard her cough a few times and worried that they would strangle her before they even crucified her. That might have been more merciful, but it broke my heart. The soldier holding the bars strained to hold her up but they also pretended to press her on like a rabid dog with their teeth gritted in the strain.

Her eyes were mostly closed. When she opened them, they looked lifeless against the remaining sunlight on the dreary day. She seemed too exhausted to show her bloodmadness, but every now and then her eyes flared with her need for blood, especially when shoved. It wasn't a physical light as portrayed in movies but rather the wild intent of a madman whose insanity lit up his eyes with too much feral energy for a sane person to muster.

A few vampires marched behind her with their hoods up and their faces concealed by the blackness that the maw of the hoods formed. However, I could recognize Richard and Lucian strictly by the way they carried their posture and walked. Even though arrogant and aristocratic, Richard was slightly slumped in defeat, but Lucian seemed enlivened at the thought of executing his rival who had killed his mate back before Abigail had been turned into a vampire.

Dexter was the only vampire who walked in front of Abigail. He had his head up with sunglasses on. He seemed to inherit Abigail's tolerance for sunlight as his hood sat back on his head exposing more of his face. He looked to be enjoying himself immensely. I wanted to punch him in his smug face almost as much as I wanted to rescue Abigail. In fact, I determined, if I was shot and dying and my handgun was empty in this crazy attempt to rescue her, my dying action would be to smash his nose flat with the gun butt.

I felt the blood drain from my face when he looked directly at me then away. He did a quick double take at me and a smile creased his arrogant face.

For a moment, I thought the jig was up, but his smile turned smug, even more smug actually. He knew that there was nothing that I could do but watch. It disheartened me more. He knew that I was powerless. As an out of towner, I could do nothing to rescue her. I, by myself, could not rally any troops to support an uprising. His eyes left me, but I could tell that he relished my ineffectuality. He was happy to let me watch helplessly. His plan was probably to kill me later at his leisure with Abigail's protection gone.

As Abigail approached, the civilians jeered, taunted and occasionally threw objects careful not to hit and infuriate a soldier. The soldiers held their professionalism somewhat better. The only show of hatred was from the men who held the metal bars that attached to her neck. They would occasionally push or prod her. When she stumbled, they would lift up on the bars, almost hanging her by the neck, causing her to cough weakly with the collar's pressure against her throat.

Seeing no way to save her in the street, I turned to leave and scope out the football field, with fear that I would only be a spectator of her torture rather than a rescuer. However as I ruminated and stepped off the curb, I felt a hand roughly grab my shoulder and force me to line back up on the side of the road with all the other jeerers. I looked up and saw a big burly soldier scowling at me.

That soldier said in a gruff voice. "Everyone is to go to the football field to witness what happens to criminals."

"That's where I was headed," I said.

"You will go with the herd after the parade passes," he barked and shoved me roughly.

I was tempted to object to a number of things including calling the townspeople a "herd." His arrogance infuriated me. However, I simply nodded my head and said, "Yes sir."

He glared at me for a second as if to see if there was any sarcasm in the way I addressed him as "sir." Sometimes I would say the word, sir, in a tone that implied an insult rather than a term of respect, but I thought that I was careful in my reply. It's hard hiding the smartass within even in the most trying of times. Maybe it is the hardest to keep it concealed, especially in the most trying of times.

When he seemed satisfied that I wasn't a smartass, he roughly shoved me again in the middle of my chest directly over my aching heart, and I watched him walk down the line of spectators. He had only walked ten feet before he started to harass another person with shoves and shouts for stepping off the curb into the street. If Josh got anywhere with his Coup d'etat, I would mention the behavior of that bully. That's if any of us even survived.

Having no choice but to stay, I watched as Abigail walked in front of me. Abigail didn't look up. Over her pale drained face her skin looked slightly burned from the short exposure to the sun on this partly cloudy winter twilight. She seemed to have no awareness other than of the men who held her bars and how they pushed her forward. I thought she would pass by oblivious to me but as she came within a few feet in front of me, her head jerked up and turned toward me with supernatural confidence in her expectation. Her vision locked on me. Her eyes were suddenly bright with urgency. She shook her head and said, "Leave town now."

A soldier gave her a violent shove through the steel bar, and she stumbled on.

"Shut up, witch!" he screamed at her.

Her face went blank as if she never saw me. I wanted to speak up for her, but I didn't dare. I wanted to yell at the soldier, not to strike a woman, but when I opened my mouth, nothing came out. I was paralyzed with cowardice at the overwhelming odds against us.

After she passed, the soldiers then herded us in the direction that the procession was headed. Those of us on the curb joined the mob of people already following Abigail and her escort through the streets.

I quickly lost sight of Abigail in the crowd of humanity, and continued to follow the flow. I grudgingly admitted that "herd" was indeed an appropriate appellation for this mob. I eagerly listened to the conversation around me. Everyone spoke in hushed tones about the return of Captain Josh Righter. I either heard it spoken of in a positive tone or with dread. Not that they didn't revere him, but rather they feared he would stir up a wasp nest of The Specter's wrath. I reasoned that if Josh did indeed attempt to pull something off this evening, it had better be one hell of a show of force. Enough to convince everyone that The Specter would be permanently declawed and defanged, if not killed, otherwise any action by Josh would be simply seen as a provocation that would only bring complete destruction to the small town.

On the walk to the football field, I tried to casually get within earshot of as many groups of people as possible to hear as many opinions as possible. It was all the same. Everybody liked Josh, the only difference was the degree of fear that they held for the possible repercussions.

The only other topic of conversation was the coming public execution, of course. I heard no one speak favorably of the vampiress. They truly believed that she alone was behind all the death caused by the vampires.

If I attempted to save her in front of the crowd, I would be torn to shreds. Too many people had lost loved ones to the bloodsuckers. The only variance in the discussion that I overheard was that some people believed executing Abigail would end the scourge of the vampires and others believed that Richard and the others should be killed as well.

The sun had just set when I arrived at the football field and the fires of the torches that blazed, added a flickering red ambiance to the already unsettling experience. Usually, campfires gave me a balming feeling of homeliness. Other times, when emotions and terrors ran wild, the flickering red flames took on an element of hell on earth. This was one of the nights for hell. As the execution neared, faces became twisted, enraged, and toothily gleeful with the carnal desire for the deadly show in the flickering flame light. Old church ladies beamed with malevolence shining in their eyes, rivaling that of the bloodmadness of the vampires at a spectacle that was a mockery of their faith. Boys ran around with toy guns shouting about killing the vampiress as they shouted, "Pow pow!" "Bang bang!" I felt that people were casting suspicious stares at me when our eyes met because I didn't return that sickening glee, but I didn't have the energy to even act like I was part of the crowd. It strained me just to follow the mob.

The town did have a small amount of electric power from alternative sources, but they were all turned off and no electric lights were used. I had an unsettling feeling that the torchlight was chosen for the purpose of adding a mythical medieval hysteria that I had already noticed.

The mob that I followed filled the bleachers around the field. There was standing room in the field close to the execution site. I planned to go there eventually to make my move, if I could but presently, I followed the group that I was currently with and walked up a couple rows in the bleachers to get a view of the execution area to make a plan for rescue. I had an idea of what to expect, however I felt a pain in my chest and abdomen that had to rival what Craig had felt when his dope was thrown in the fire. I almost collapsed with the weight of hopelessness and fear as I looked at Abigail's cross as she was forced to walk to it. It was laying on the ground in wait for her willowy form.

Although I wasn't the most religious person by any means, I had been raised in a nominally Christian household. To me, I had always seen a cross as less of an ancient torture device, but rather a symbol of freedom from our most nightmarish images of death, slavery, and intimidation. It had lost its horror for me that it would have held over people who lived in ancient Roman times. However to see a bare cross lying waiting to torture to death a person who I had a great affection for, especially as a scapegoat for the crimes that others had committed, not her. In the past, a cross was a sign to me of triumph over death. Here it was a symbol of death triumphing over the innocent woman who I loved even if I could never fully commit to her because we were almost technically different species.

"Abigail…" Just whispering her name hit me like a blow to the solar plexus. I held onto a railing on the bleachers and almost collapsed.

"Get a grip," I muttered to myself.

On that impromptu stage by the bare cross, I saw a row of men in birdlike gas masks that purposely were reminiscent of doctors during the ancient plaques. They wore the black paramilitary uniforms and the long flowing capes like the vampires. Despite their monstrous appearance, they were fully human. These were The Specter's personal guard from the Safe Zone. To violate the seal of their mask was to forever banish them to the Forbidden Zone. Because of this, they tended to shoot if you even approached within ten feet of them to prevent exposure to any of the viruses in the Forbidden Zone. They were given that power, and worst of all, they seemed to revel in it behind the inhuman glare of their mask's glassy goggles.

"Are you alright, buddy?" a man with a low but nasal voice asked.

I let go of the railing and didn't even look at the man who addressed me. I stood upright. My legs were strong. It was not a phony show of strength. I resolved at that moment that she would not die in such a disgraceful manner, even if I had to put a mercy bullet in her head, but I determined that I wouldn't have to resort to that. I was taking her out of town alive. I had to. I just didn't know how at the moment.

"Think, Eric," I muttered to myself.

A crowd had gathered around me as if concerned that I was about to pass out. Maybe they were concerned that I was muttering to myself. Afterall, people regularly went insane these days. Talking to oneself was also a sign of succumbing to a zombie's bite. I'm sure some people were itching to kill me if I showed any sign of succumbing to the zombie disease.

I looked them firmly in the eyes, and then I replied to the man with the deep nasal voice who had initially expressed his concern, "Yes. I am fine. I just slipped on the steps."

All eyes went back to the cross as Abigail approached it.

The crowd seemed to vibrate with the rumble of thousands of conversations and excitement. I heard the man with the low nasal voice ask me something more, but I was already moving down the steps of the bleachers against the crowd to the front of the spectator's section in the standing area before Abigail's cross.

On the field, everybody pressed forward to get a better view or to hear the screams of Abigail when the torture began. It turned my stomach. It was one thing to attend an execution where one's presence was mandatory. It was another thing to get closer for enjoyment. This aspect of mankind sickened me. Having seen death, I no longer had a morbid sense of curiosity. I prayed some were getting closer with the goal of ending and killing The Specter, like me, but I wasn't relying on that. Bryan told me to have faith in God or fate if one didn't believe in deities, but never in your fellow man. I didn't want to write off the virtue and strength in my friends, but feeling the sick sensation in my belly and weakness in my heart, I knew he was right. Because, as a person myself, I feared that no one could depend upon me. Not Abigail nor even myself.

"Abigail..."

I left the bleachers and stepped onto the grassy field. I pushed forward, squeezing through any opening that I saw and making openings by insinuating myself through where there were none with my insistence and pressing shoulder. I ignored verbal protests and if someone pushed me from behind or my side, I used that momentum to push myself ever closer.

I shivered as I heard The Specter's rumbling voice cut through the chaotic chatter of the crowd. I could see the skull-faced man on the slight rise of dirt where the execution would occur, but I wanted to be at the very front so that I could act when needed. I didn't believe that I could do anything against all the powers and people of the Forbidden Zone, but I had to at least show up.

I pushed and squeezed my way through the final crush of four or five more lines of people. With a savage curse, someone behind me gave a vicious shove, and I slammed through the remaining people and into the hastily erected metal fence. It came up to my navel, so I squatted slightly so that those behind me could be a witness to the coming perversions without getting any more curses verbally thrown at me for blocking the view.

I saw the vampires around the Specter walking down an aisle to the small rise where the cross lay. They had removed their hoods as the night had fallen. Night was their dawn. Dexter walked, leering at Abigail. I felt some of the paralyzing fear in my gut get pushed away by the ferocious need to end his life. I could hear David's chant in my head, "Kill! Kill! Kill!" Although it had been mostly silent since the hot bath back at the camp, it was loud as a harsh whisper, but I cursed its alien presence in my head. They halted at the cross as The Specter kept speaking. They surrounded Abigail, and kept her on her feet. She weakly stood with her eyes closed.

My gut dropped as Richard scanned the crowd. His eyes stopped when they met my own. We stared deep as if judging each others' strength by the will alone that showed in our eyes. He diverted his stare to look at The Specter. For a panicked moment I was sure that he was about to report me, but instead his eyes returned to my own. There was nothing but sadness. Defeat. Richard cared as much for Abigail as I did, but in a fatherly way. I didn't know which of us felt more pain. He had a chance to kill me last night but withheld his bullet because he knew that it would break Abigail's heart.

Richard looked at me with a clenched jaw and then lowered his gaze, always avoiding looking at Dexter. I could tell that he felt as powerless as me. He then looked back up at me and we shared that moment of heartfelt commiseration.

I don't know why I felt it, but I had a feeling that Richard was being deposed, replaced as the head of the vampires by Dexter.

The Specter raised his black leather clad fists into the air in a sign of victory for the entire town of Craigsville. The people around me cheered wildly.

The Specter shouted, "People of Craigsville! Tonight, I bring an end to the terror of the vampires with the death of their criminal. After tonight, we will begin a new alliance with the vampires. They shall aid in our defense from the zombies. The defeat of Abigail and our victory is within sight! Have faith in me! The scourge of zombism is nigh and shall end as well with their help!"

I hated to concede that The Specter's booming voice and announcement was stirring. If I did not have the inside knowledge that I had, I might have gotten caught up and cheered as well. We all wanted an end to the terrors, and the power of his voice seemed to shake the ground beneath my feet and even into my soul. For me, knowing that he was an inspirational liar was heart crushing. For the townspeople he was motivating.

People around me pressed in against the barrier as if wishing to be nearer to him, but no one dared to violate it with the bird masked soldiers who guarded him.

There were a lot of cheers around me. However there was also a lot of grumbling as well. I had a flash of regret that I didn't stay in the bleachers. That way I would have a better panoramic view to strategize and probably be around a lot more people who I could rally to resist The Specter. Only the sickos were drawing near, in my opinion. Those who wished to overthrow the tyrannical bastard stayed far away, I thought.

The Specter continued on a little longer. I was starting to get nervous and my mind seemed to shut out everything around me. I no longer heard words, only the rumble of The Specter's inhumanly deep voice.

I knew that Josh's original plan was to attack when all the attention was on The Specter and hopefully channel the crowd's discontent at an obvious enemy who wears a skull mask and scares children, women and even the most hardened of soldiers with the mere mention of his name. I was hoping it would all go down before the execution began, but as time slipped away, I began to fear that he was waiting for the execution itself as the signal. A crucifixion would be the ultimate distraction for the coup d'etat. The vampiress hanging for everyone's attention was perfect for his plans. The death of a vampire, even Abigail, was easily worth the sacrifice to him. It is what I would have done had I not known Abigail and if my sole goal was to free the town of my birth. A thousand residents who consisted of family and boyhood friends would be more important than the life of a vampiress. I hated his decision, but couldn't blame him.

Another fear hit me, what if Josh was killed during his earlier escape attempt? What if he could gather no one to support him? Josh was brave, but he was not as impulsive as Douglas. He held no allegiance to Abigail, and probably disliked the vampiress strictly on principle. When faced with a crowd of monsters, it's hard when running in fear to distinguish the good from the bad ones. I remembered my own parting insult and threat to her just last night.

I looked at Abigail. She was the sole reason why I was here. I was hoping that looking at her would give me some inspiration, but all it did was fill me with hopelessness. She was still standing upright, held in place by two other vampires and the soldier holding the bars. She didn't even have the strength to hold her head up. Her chin rested on her chest. Her neck was so bowed that it looked unnatural and uncomfortable. The rest of her body seemed to sink into the hands of the other vampires who held her up by her armpits.

"Abigail," I whispered silently.

Somehow over the roar of the crowd and the booming speech of The Specter, she heard my muttered whisper. She lifted her eyes. Her eyes were clear as if too exhausted to hold the feral madness of the desire for blood.

"Abigail," I whispered again.

She stared at me and seemingly with her last ounce of strength, her lips muttered, "Shoot me. Don't give them the pleasure of my crucifixion."

I doubt that any sound came from her lips, but I heard her clearly in my mind. I was surprised when my hand gripped the pistol that was holstered in my belt as if someone else controlled it.

She was less than ten meters away. Technically, it would be an easy shot to kill her with a head shot, but the physics of aiming was useless if the heart rebels. I didn't know if I could calm the shakes in my hands to take a good aim at her.

Her eyes lit up with energy from an unknown well in her soul. "Do it!" she commanded in my head.

I felt a surge of willpower to finish her. I suspected mind control and something instinctively inside me knew that was the case, but that mind control didn't come from her. I looked at Richard. His eyes bore into my own.

"If you don't, I will," I clearly heard him but his lips didn't move.

So despite the psychic control supposedly being knocked out, the vampires still had some psionic powers, I realized.

Although normally, I would rebel against any mind control, but in this case, I let his willpower be my own. With their weakened powers, it wasn't much but I decided to use his influence to help my actions. I unsnapped my holster and started to draw. My focus returned to Abigail, whose head had slumped and rested on her chest again. With Richard's help, I believed that I could shoot her if her soulful eyes didn't look at me.

"Kill, kill, kill," I heard David command from the grave. I allowed his voice to grow louder.

I heard Abigail quietly say in my head, "Thank you Eric. I have always loved you."

"I have always loved you, too," I thought back at her.

I took a breath. My handgun cleared the holster. I told myself that I would raise it quickly and as soon as the front site was on her head I would squeeze the trigger. Then I would shoot The Specter and then Dexter. I blew the pent up air out of my lungs and started to bring the weapon to bear on her, but I stopped before it was raised above my navel.

I heard some soldiers behind me speaking in hushed tones as The Specter droned on, I listened and distinctly heard one man say, "I'm slaying that skull faced ass myself, when Josh launches the signal." I assumed he was a soldier by his confident masculine voice as well as his spoken intentions.

I kept facing forward pretending that I didn't hear anything. As casually as I could, I replaced the handgun in its holster. Maybe there was hope. I knew Richard probably wasn't happy but I avoided eye contact and mentally blocked the section of my mind where he would try to control or influence me.

I heard the others soldiers around the first soldier agree as they quietly discussed their coming plan of action. I didn't hear everything, but I knew that if Josh didn't do something fast, I could make a move and initiate the battle myself.

Then I felt my hopes shatter like a glass bottle on concrete.

I heard the voice of the man who said that he would kill The Specter himself say, "Oh hell no. I ain't making no move now."

"Yeah, that's out of the question," one of his comrades wholeheartedly agreed.

I turned around and faced them. I wasn't surprised to see that the men who I had been eavesdropping on were soldiers of Craigville in the black paramilitary uniform. At least three of them held my eye contact with me as I pinned them with a withering glare.

"Cowards!" I hissed.

I stared at them unsure of why they suddenly changed their minds. They sounded so sure of themselves just seconds ago. They returned my glare levelly. They weren't cowards.

Then I heard a steady, "whomp whomp," that seemed to start in my chest and the beat of it squeezed my heart with each concussive thump as it reached my ears.

I closed my eyes suddenly feeling thoroughly defeated as I realized why they backed out. There was no way any of them would attack The Specter with the helicopters circling. I counted at least four choppers now above the crowds. Two Blackhawks and two Apaches. The lights of the aircrafts blazed brightly. I saw the bristling turrets of the machine guns and the pods for rocket launchers. There was nothing the town could do against them.

I felt so defeated that I heard the men mocking my bravado but couldn't comprehend any distinct words. However I did hear one of them laugh about the way my face slumped at the sound of the warbirds above us. I couldn't blame them.

Josh and his men were brave, but not suicidal. Saving a vampire wasn't a top priority for anyone in this town, especially for Josh who was once supposed to be fed to those beasts. They could simply wait for another day.

I couldn't wait. I had to do something but what?

Half the crowd applauded something that The Specter proclaimed with his massively muscular arms spread as wide as pterodactyl wings. I missed what he said, but he had an engaging personality. He could have been a motivational speaker in another life.

"You like that?" The Specter proclaimed.

Some more cheering greeted his words.

"It shall become my crusade to wipe out all the vampires who prey upon your loved ones, but every journey begins with a step, and every vanquishing of evil begins with one crucified vampire. So let us begin!"

Half the crowd cheered. The other half just watched with rapt attention, and then like zombies the quiet ones began to applaud to join the others who were already clapping.

I felt a hand on my shoulder and turned to see the man who had boasted about killing The Specter himself. He leaned in and shouted into my ear above the roar of the applause, "I respect your guts, man. I thought you were just talking, but you were about to jump the fence. Don't do it. You'll be cut down before you get halfway to that monster. I have seen it before."

I nodded, thinking about Douglas, but my focus was on The Specter as he shouted, "Bring the vampiress to the cross!"

The four men holding the four steel poles guided Abigail toward The Specter and the cross. They all wore thick leather gloves and arm gauntlets to prevent the danger of a bite. Once they made it to the cross, I watched Dexter walk forward and unlocked the steel ring around her neck. The soldiers stepped away cautiously. Abigail stood on unsteady legs like a newborn foal for a moment, but just as she collapsed, The Specter grabbed her by the front of her black hooded cloak and steadied her.

Richard, Lucian and four other vampires followed. Their hoods were down. Richard was somber as were the others except Lucian. The young vampire looked downright giddy. Richard's face suddenly shifted. His eyes bored straight into mine again. His face was stoney. He furrowed his brow and I feared he would betray me. However he looked away again.

Although I didn't trust him in the slightest, I prayed that he would be even a temporary ally. I looked away from him, back to Abigail.

The Specter held her in a standing position with one arm as he yanked off her cloak with his other arm. Beneath the cloak she wore only black pants and a black T-shirt over her willowy athletic body. I feared that he would strip her naked to add to her indignity. I was grateful when he didn't, but she seemed to be too out of it from the blood loss to realize. I guessed that The Specter did it simply so she wouldn't die too quickly from the cold. Her face indeed looked pale and icy. She said without blood she would die before midnight whether she was crucified or not. I grimly remembered how cold her skin felt as I held her hands through the bars in the dungeon.

She could offer no resistance, as he pushed her down over the logs that formed the "t" shape. Even if I rescued her, she couldn't help in the fight against our enemies or even run. I would have to carry her, if I even got that far.

I watched in horror as two soldiers rolled up her pants legs. They didn't remove her boots. I guessed that the leather of the thigh high boots would offer no resistance to the ten inch nails. I feared inaction before. Now I feared that I could not control my actions as I watched one soldier slap her across the face with a rough laugh to rouse her enough to feel the pain.

The other two soldiers stretched her arms across the cross beam. The Specter produced a long nail and a hammer from a pocket of his cloak. He placed the point of the ten inch nail on her wrist. The vampiress only had enough strength to roll her head to avert her gaze from the hammer and nail. Abigail then screamed as the hammer tinked on the nail and drove it through her forearm just above her wrist. It was a tired croaking scream. No blood poured out of the wound from her already drained body.

However, her cries triggered something deep inside me. I heard the soldier who spoke of killing The Specter yell at me, "No, man! Don't!"

It was only then that I realized that I impulsively jumped the fence. I could not stand idly by and watch. It was impossible for me at that moment. My sword was in my hand. Of course, I didn't think it through. I don't know why I drew my sword rather than my handgun. There were many good reasons to stick with my sword. One of course was the zombies. Two, if I opened fire and they fired back, I would instantly be cut down, but with a sword, I could at least make it to The Specter as the others would stick with quieter weapons until things got too chaotic.

However, there was no conscious reasoning in me. Maybe Richard worked some mental power on me. Regardless, savage instinct drove me and I simply attacked!

"Kill! Kill! Kill!" David screamed from the beyond, and that was the rhythm of my slashing blade as I attacked.

I attacked The Specter's bird beaked soldiers who stood guard along the fence. Despite the chilling effect that their appearance had on people, their biowarfare masks hindered their ability to fight, and I sliced right through two of the men and sprinted past the line up the slight rise. The Specter hammered the nail one more time, sinking it into the hard wood of the cross. He then turned to see why the crowd erupted in a strange mixture of cheers, boos, and hisses. I hoped the crowd would be driven by my rash decision and join, otherwise, my fight would be a brief one.

"Hildebrande!" The Specter roared, staring into my crazed eyes as I charged at him. He dropped the hammer and drew his sword. His black cloak flew out as he spun to face me. His sword was halfway out of the scabbard as I slashed at his hand. I smashed my sword into the hilt of his. His sword flew out of his hands but I missed his wrist where I was aiming. I cursed as I had wanted to dismember the bastard.

I brought my sword up to cleave his skull as two of the bird faced, gas masked men attacked me with their own blades. My sword got hung up in their swords while defending myself, and we grimly locked pushing our blades against each other. I only had one goal in mind, so I dropped the sword and charged straight at The Specter. I had no fear, only a desire to see what was behind the mask that had haunted my nightmare scapes. I launched myself at him as he bent to retrieve his sword.

I hoped that demasking him would change the mood of the crowd, to show either the monstrosity or humanity beneath.

From the corner of my eye I saw Richard raise his vampiric sword as I impacted into The Specter. I didn't strike The Specter however. I slammed bodily into him as my hand reached for his mask. I missed the mask and turned my grab into a punch as he bent. Because of his awkward position he fell to the ground and we both rolled, fighting for dominance as I reached for his face. My fingernails raked at The Specter's eyes, as I expected Richard's sword to cleave my skull at any moment.

I screamed in savage victory as I grasped his skull mask and yanked. The Specter wound up on top as I ripped the mask off and flung it at the crowd. Everyone gasped as they saw his bare face. He was fully human. His personal guard hesitated at the violation and worst of all, I recognised the son of a bitch who was sitting on my chest.

Enragement flooded my veins as we stared at each other. I was in a state of both shock and fury. The Specter was none other than Don Renton. My former friend Tommy's right hand man. The man who bullied me, threatened my life at gunpoint, and literally kicked me off the helicopter, unarmed, into the horrors of the Forbidden Zone. I roared and despite the larger man's size, the fire in my heart sent him rolling off of me as I bucked my hips. We both rolled to our feet and I savagely attacked him with punch after punch. I aimed at his temple where I could see the stitches that still remained when I pistol whipped him just last week.

Don Renton stared at me in fear for a moment after being unmasked. His fear fed my confidence and rage as he leapt to his feet with me following the much bigger man.

I caught sight of Richard as he slashed at the soldier's throat who had been holding Abigail down. Blood poured as the soldier collapsed to the ground at the cross.

The crowd howled and surged against the fence but stayed behind as they watched the events unfold. I picked up my sword and readied it for a fight.

Blood ran down The Specter's face from where I punched at his stitched up head as he backed away from my furious approach. I was after his blood and the crowd, seeing him as a mortal, bellowed for his death now.

"Eric!" I looked behind me as the vampiress called me. One of the bird faced men swung at my head with a sword and I barely dodged the slash by moving to the side. I saw her eyes light as if on fire as she screamed, yanking her arm against the nail that protruded halfway out of her wrist. The Specter only hit the nail twice and it wasn't in the wood very deeply. Her arm and the nail came free. She grabbed the nail in her other hand and threw it. The point of the nail impacted into a soldier's head as he was swinging his sword at me for a follow up causing him to collapse and stay down. I didn't see if it penetrated his skull, but I looked at Abigail. The fire had left her eyes and she slumped back on the cross as if dead. The throw of the spike exhausted her bloodless and drained body.

The strength in that woman, I marveled.

The soldiers, vampires, and The unmasked Specter, then surrounded Richard, the supine Abigail, and me. We were horribly outnumbered. There was no way that the three of us could fight our way out of this. Even Lucian grinned as he pointed a sword at my heart. Dexter was nowhere in sight.

An Apache helicopter approached and hovered above us. It's guns aimed at the three of us. The enemies stepped back to let the chopper do its deeds.

The chopper's loudspeaker bellowed, "Lay down your swords, now!"

It was either lay down our swords and surrender or go out in a blaze. I expected no mercy from Don Renton. As I steeled my legs as springs for one final leap at him, I saw what I thought was a firework that some pervert set off to celebrate the execution, but it streaked as a fireball with a long tail and smashed into the Apache that was aiming its guns at me. Immediately after the impact, the Apache exploded and plummeted in a fiery swan dive smashing into a line of opposing soldiers within thirty meters of me. The ground shook so violently that I almost fell to the ground,

"Yeah, Critter," I said to myself and coughed on the smoke from the fiery wreckage that immediately covered the field. A few secondary explosions blew from the Apache's munitions detonating. Shrapnel screamed over my head and then deadly debris rained around me.

I smiled as I saw another fiery chopper fall from the sky in the distance and the remaining two choppers quickly turned tail and flew away followed by a fiery streak that impacted one of the remaining Apaches, sending it smashing into the Earth in an explosive fury.

Fired up by the three choppers shot out of the sky, the crowd jumped the fence to attack Don Renton and his soldiers.

I looked around the flames and saw Don Renton run and disappear into the darkened, smoky night. I sheathed my sword and slung an M-16 from a dead soldier over my shoulder, I grabbed another one and pocketed a few loaded magazines I was about to sprint after Don fueled by predatory intent. My heart was full of desire to end his tyrannical reign, when I heard Richard scream, "Eric."

The sense of urgency and the shrieking roar only a vampire could muster in the senior vampire's voice caused me to pause my pursuit. I turned to look at him. He stood strong in protection of his vampiric daughter as a semicircle of ten of Craigsville's soldiers surrounded him. He stood by will alone, holding them from attacking Abigail. His defense wouldn't last long as I could see he was already wounded by sword slices in quite a few places.

The head vampire yelled, "Get Abigail out of here. I will hold them off and follow."

I knew he was making a sacrificial final stand and wouldn't follow. The ten soldiers advanced. I thought he would be inundated, but he flashed his fangs in the explosive firelight and half roared, half hissed at them. The sight of the aristocratic middle aged man suddenly turning into a monster stopped them in their tracks.

"Go!" he roared at me. His eyes blazed at me in a fury that actually terrified me to obey. I couldn't tell if it was supernatural or the reflection from the fire of the downed Apache that lit his eyes, but they glowed as fiery as the detonating helicopters with his rage.

I ran to Abigail. "Come on," I yelled urgently at her as I tried to pull her off the cross and to her feet, but her arm was limp, eyelids fluttering with semi consciousness. Richard had earlier draped her black hooded cloak over her for warmth. I bent down and buttoned the neck catch and slung her over my shoulder in a fireman's carry.

With the weapons and Abigail on my shoulder, I was a bit awkward. I sprinted in the direction that The Specter took. At this moment my only goal was to escape, not to finish my fight with Don Renton, however, that was the only route of escape open to me. The field before me was filled with enemies who wanted Abigail dead, but in the night under the pall of smoke and confusion of battle, I was able to make a sprint. Visibility was only measured by a few feet at the most. Most people were bent over coughing on smoke, giving me the edge that I needed.

I coughed on the oily smoke from the burning Apache, but was grateful for its cover as I ignored my urge to stop and bend over to hack up a lung. I could pretty much only see people when I almost blindly bumped off of them. They were just trying to escape the wreckage of the choppers as munitions kept exploding. I winced each time something exploded. Some of the debris from the detonating Apache screamed over my head at lethal speed. Some of the other man-killing wreckage rained down near me crashing into the dirt. I heard a few people cry out with shrapnel wounds. Bedlam was the only rule at that moment.

With the vampiress on my shoulder, I sprinted down the gravel road taken by Don Renton. I peeked over my shoulder and saw Richard flooded by soldiers through a gap in the smoke and lit by a sudden detonation of the apache's armament. He collapsed under the flashing swords and they hacked at him. They looked up from the mutilated, and I am sure, dead vampire and called for me to halt. That caused me to sprint faster.

Fifty yards behind me, they chased after me with their swords, instinctively following the no firearm rule for fear of drawing zombies. That was ridiculous because the explosion from the crashing choppers and stinger missiles were much louder than any rifle report, but clear thinking went out the window in the pandemonium. I had a slight lead, but carrying Abigail's unconscious weight slowed me down and they were rapidly gaining.

I rounded a corner as I hit the streets and was out of their sight for the merest of moments. I plunged into a hedgerow along a brick building. The row of bushes stood about two feet over my head. I muffled a curse as thorns dug into my exposed flesh as I pushed my way through the hedge. I wasn't sure what the shrub was, but I hated it with all my guts. Still, I powered through as the sticky branches seemed to try to restrain me. After a few feet, I arrived at the brick building of the school.

There was a clear spot between the hedge and the brick wall. I used to make these clear areas between a shrub row and a building as forts when I was a kid. It gave me an odd feeling of safety now from the nostalgia. I forgave the plant for stabbing me with its thorns.

I squatted down and listened to the squad of soldiers race past my position. When it appeared that they wouldn't backtrack to see if I was hiding, I set Abigail's body down. I checked her vitals, and was relieved to see that her chest still rose and collapsed with her breath, but they were gasping breaths as if her lungs were reaching desperately for air. I then sat next to her and waited for things to quiet down.

I could walk out and probably avoid suspicion on my own, but not with a vampiress over my shoulder. I was tempted to throw away her black hooded cloak that was a uniform of anyone working for The Specter, particularly the vampires, but the chill in the air was below freezing and Abigail's lips were blue from a lack of blood and the cold. I touched the soft skin of her face with the back of my hand and it felt colder than the icy night's air. If not for her labored breathing and the amazing regenerative properties inherent to vampires, I would have left her. Even if she died right here, I felt a form of vindication that they didn't get a chance to publicly humiliate and torture her. However, although barely, she still breathed and I had hope that we could still escape.

I took off her cloak and placed my coat on her and then replaced her cloak over it.

I wasn't sure how exactly the vampiress' metabolism worked, but I had felt her radiant body heat when we leaned against each other in the Cave of the Nunnehi and almost kissed as we looked over the cliff. Now, she felt deathly cold. I knew that wasn't good.

I suddenly heard gunfire erupt in the center of town about a quarter mile away from me. I guessed that it was fighting near the Headquarters building. I hoped that it was Josh. Everything else around me was quiet, so I replaced Abigail on my shoulder and after looking for a relatively thornless passage out of the hedge, I gave up and pushed my way through and ignored the pain. It was worse without the protection of the coat that I had put on Abigail

I jogged at a light pace unchallenged with the woman over my shoulder and quickly arrived at the dilapidated white barn. My goal was to hole up, but I remembered the tunnel system and the secondary passage that led in the direction of the mountains, where I wished to escape from the town. I checked the coordinates on the compass to make sure it did jive when I went down there. I didn't want to try an unknown passage, but I kept that knowledge in the back of my head.

I entered the barn and slid the bolt to lock the barn's door behind me with the plan to wait until things quieted down and simply walk out of Craigsville, above ground..

After the door clicked shut, I heard soldiers shouting in urgent tones outside, "I saw him!"

I scowled and opened the hatch into the tunnel. I wasn't about to enter it, but I wanted it open, just in case.

I froze as I heard a voice outside the barn say, "Yes, sir! I saw him come in here with the vampiress over his shoulder."

A fist thudded like gunshots on the door. So thunderous, that I thought the rotted wood would implode under the forceful knocks.

"Open up, Hildebrande!" I heard The Specter/Don Renton command.

"Go to hell! Bastard!" I screamed back.

I grimly realized that the man beast still had power over a good number of Craigsville's soldiers as they pounded on the door.

| 17 |

They futilely tried the door handle as I lifted Abigail over my shoulder, and I climbed down the dark passage. Then bullets slammed into the door and whistled around my head as I started to go down. I quickly ducked beneath the opening.

I heard a crash against the door, and The Specter/Don Renton grunt and then yell with rage. I could tell that he had pounded his foot or shoulder against the bolted door.

It barely held and then a second blow caused it to explode inward. Wooden splinters followed me down the hole.

I tried to close the hatch, but couldn't while trying not to fall off the decrepit ladder as well as holding the vampiress. I only managed to half cover it and left it to climb down the rest of the ladder. I started to run as soon as my boots hit the mud, splashing through the dank passage in pitch black and bounced off the unforgiving walls a few times.

"Hang in there Abigail," I encouraged her limp body on my shoulder.

She didn't answer but I could feel her muscles moving slightly in response to my running. It wasn't much, but she was still alive.

I had only gone about twenty yards when I heard the trap door fully open and soon after boots splashing in the muddy water behind me.

"They had to go down here. There's nowhere else to go," I heard the echoing voice of a soldier.

"Go!" boomed Don Renton.

Stooped over, I started running faster. The passage wound a bit and I could see a vague luminescence of a flashlight bouncing off the stone walls behind me. I flicked my own light on. I worried that they could see mine, but I kept mine on for fear of missing the side passage. I did not want to end up at headquarters with a condemned vampiress on my shoulder.

The next voice echoed through the tunnel and the enclosed space made it sound like he shouted in my ear. "I can hear him splashing, come on!"

"I see his light," shouted another.

"It's him with the vampire on his shoulder!" someone shouted in victory.

I saw the side passage thirty yards ahead of me and shut off my light as bullets whistled by me in the enclosed space, but thankfully, I rounded a slight bend in the passage and was temporarily safe as I kept running.

I almost passed by the side passage, but I had my hand feeling the cold damp stone wall. I stopped and sprinted in it as bullets whistled past me. It was hard running stooped over in the low ceilinged passage with the weight of a body on the shoulder. I checked a compass on my jacket's lapel and indeed I was headed in the right direction toward the mountains in the northern corner of the town. I hoped that this mysterious passage would take me out of the town rather than ending up in a bad spot in the middle of the action.

I rounded a sharp corner that gave me solid cover and heard someone yell, "He's gone down this side passage."

I fired my handgun down the passage and cursed. The blast in the confined space almost deafened me, but I heard one of the soldiers yelp in pain.

"The bastard hit me!"

They fired back and the lead splatted into the wall right next to me, but the bend in the passage shielded me. I fired around the corner. Another man cried out in pain. Someone shined a bright light in my direction and I fired at the source. Another scream rewarded my shot.

A heavy barrage of bullets slammed into the wall next to me, but I was protected as I ducked back behind the stone corner.

I yelled at them, "I can stay here all day. You can't hit me and I will kill anyone who steps into the passage."

Some more bullets slammed into the wall beside me.

I forced myself to laugh at them.

"I can stay here all night, dumbasses!" I taunted.

"Dammit!" Renton's curse was almost as loud as the gunfire. "Where does this damn tunnel lead?"

A flunky answered his master, "We don't know sir. None of us knew that any of these tunnels existed until now."

All the bullets that they fired had hit at chest level on the exposed wall to my right, so I set Abigail down behind the wall and got in the prone position. Instantly the front of my clothes were damp. When my opponents opened fire, I sent a barrage back from around the corner and was rewarded with another scream of agony and a curse from Renton. The passage funneled my bullets with a devastating effect. They would not try to charge me, but I was low on bullets.

Don Renton bellowed, "Go to headquarters and search the archives. Find out where this damned tunnel leads. I want to cut him off!"

I half grinned. I had really rattled Renton. He was shouting his plans loud enough for me to hear. He was a man used to commanding absolute control and now that was slipping away and he was unnerved and was losing control of what mattered the most, his mind.

My grin disappeared. I didn't know how the fighting was going above. I had no idea where this tunnel ended. Worst of all, I didn't know if Abigail would make it.

I fired again, but hit no one. They returned fire, this time aiming lower at my gun blasts. I backed around the corner. They weren't going to follow me into this lead funnel anytime soon. I then scooted back further as I heard them in a heated discussion, and picked up Abigail. I quietly walked down the passage, hoping to find a good exit beyond the town.

After a few hundred meters, I began to quietly run for another ten minutes through the passage. My fear was running into a dead end or even worse, emerging into a barracks of soldiers. Whether friendly to Josh or not, everyone in town, except me, wanted the vampiress dead.

Eventually, I came to what looked like a dead end. I pushed around and the rock wall pivoted into a small chamber. An old wooden ladder bolted to the wall with rusted nails reached eighteen feet for the stone ceiling. I climbed, fearing each step on the decrepit ladder would send me and Abigail plummeting to the ground, but it held creakingly, barely. I reached the top and pushed on the stone door above me and my heart sank. It wouldn't budge.

I felt around and found a latch. I pulled it and heard an ancient rusted metal bolt grind, click, and then grind some more. I pushed the stone and it moved. It was heavy and I feared the extra weight would shatter one of the ladder rungs that I was standing on. I was tempted to go back down the ladder and drop off Abigail and climb back up to get some leverage without her weight. However, I managed to push the stone door to the side. I gave one last lunge, causing the rung I was standing on to break. I barely caught myself and clung to Abigail. The trap door moved with enough space to escape the tunnel with her still on my shoulder. I cursed as another rotted rung under my foot gave way, and I barely found a foothold on the remaining metal peg that had bolted the broken rung to the wall. I held on and scrambled to the next rung and out.

I gratefully breathed in the fresh air as I luxuriated in the mountainous forest around me. I was free for the moment and just on the other side of the wall defending Craigsville. I was tempted to place the vampiress on the ground to rest, but three zombies shambled at me. Their nostrils flaring with my scent. I pocketed my weakening flashlight and drew my sword with one hand as I still held Abigail on my shoulder in a fireman's carry. I sliced the first and second one's heads off with a single slash, splashing the night with zombie goo in the light of the moon and stars. The third one was almost on me as I slashed down lodging the blade into its rib cage at the junction of the shoulder and the neck, severing its spine just below the throat.

I twisted and yanked the sword out on the third try. I scolded myself for swinging the last stroke like a baseball bat rather than slashing like a sword. That's what wedged it in the bones. If there had been a fourth zombie, it could have spelled the end for me

Catching my breath, I looked around. Abigail and I were alone. I briefly congratulated myself. Two weeks ago, I didn't think I could slay a zombie or a vampire. Now I had slain three zombies while I carried a vampiress that I rescued on my shoulder. The future is made to be altered and shattered, I thought.

I put Abigail down and replaced the hatch over the tunnel. I was in the woods and the hatch looked like any other random stone. I weighed it down with a few large rocks to make sure no one could open it to pursue me. I then walked to the abandoned car and recovered the weapons and the pack I had left inside earlier in the day. I had been extremely lucky that the tunnel ended where it did.

I breathed in deeply to replenish my reserves and rolled my painful shoulders before lifting her again. I took off in a jog up the steep mountain slope carrying Abigail. She was a slim, athletic woman but she had some mass from strong muscles and was relatively tall, but I pushed myself carrying her up the steep slope through the brush. It was a noisy push up the hill, I didn't have time to look for the trail.

After a few hundred yards of sprinting up the mountain, I stopped and looked down at the town. I saw a confident figure that could be no one else but Captain Josh Righter standing on the front porch of the gothic southern mansion that served as headquarters for the town of Craigsville. Lines of soldiers in formation listened to words that I couldn't hear. I was glad to see that he was succeeding.

After catching some of my breath, I continued to run up the hill, ironically to get away from other people rather than vampires or zombies.

| 18 |

A few hours later, back in Tommy's office, Don Renton leaned back in a plush leather recliner staring at the ceiling where his toes pointed. An icepack rested over his forehead and his massive hand covered the pack and balanced it giving the appearance that he pondered very dire consequences. Although his mask was off, he still wore the rest of his uniform. The black cloak covered the chair like a funeral shroud. However, his eyes fiercely blazed.

His face had been cleaned up but a reddish bruise that would soon discolor to a darker tone mottled his face. A small crust of overlooked dried blood slowly flaked off under his ear. He had immediately fled the town after he realized that Eric could hold him off indefinitely in the tunnel. With the choppers gone, Craig missing, and the town folk rallying with Josh against him, he ran.

Don had never run from a fight in his life. The pilot of the Blackhawk, who flew him out, was so shaken that he almost disobeyed the orders to fly back to Craigsville to rescue Don. None of the savages of the Forbidden Zone had ever dared to shoot down a warbird in the two years since it all went down.

They had been invincible until now. Don fumed in a quiet but simmering, impotent rage as the cause of his flight was from Eric, a man he seriously misjudged as a harmless geek.

Tommy and Don sat in silence trying to determine what the new turn of events meant.

Tommy finally said excitedly, "How much of Eric's footage are we uploading to the internet? That was intense, but I'm sure that we'll have to censor some of it, of course."

Tommy was focused on his job. His eyes were on his computer rather than the big man in the recliner. In his zeal to do his work to make entertaining propaganda for the masses to bring in tax revenue, he overlooked the smoldering fuse that was Don Renton's dangerous temper.

"Are you that stupid?" Don asked as if suffering from a combination of simmering rage, exhaustion, as well as a splitting headache.

Tommy ruefully shook his head as he complained, not listening to the smoldering powder keg that was Don, "Our reality show was just starting to take off."

Although Don's job was to subjugate the population, Tommy's job was to bring in revenue with the videos. People gladly paid their taxes if it came with entertainment.

Don didn't share Tommy's outlook.

The ice pack crashed into a large abstract painting on the opposite wall, exploding ice and water everywhere.

It took Tommy a moment to realize that Don had thrown it. The act was so sudden and violent. The paint ran down the picture like mascara dripping down the cheeks of a weeping widow. It smeared the painting, but oddly seemed to add to the abstract art rather than vandalizing it.

The savage throw brought Don to his feet as if ready to fight anyone in his reach. Tommy was the only other person in the room and Tommy was no fighter..

"Are you really that thick headedly stupid?" Don exclaimed, clenching his heavy fists.

"Hey," Tommy scolded, "You don't talk to me like that."

"Or what? I never truly worked for you and now that Governor Hildebrande is deposed, your days in a plush office are probably over."

Tommy stared into space as if hearing the news for the first time.

Don continued as he menacingly closed the space between them, "Did you really think that your cushy life would continue as normal?"

Tommy had considered it of course. Eric Hildebrande's uncle and adopted father, the former Governor Daniel Hildebrande had just recently been deposed in a lightning fast, almost bloodless coup. Tommy and Eric had attended a high end private school and Tommy's father had been very good friends with the up and coming senior Daniel Hildebrande. With his connections and manipulative personality, Tommy easily ascended the ranks with his connection. He brilliantly blended intelligence gathering with the entertainment industry and found himself as a celebrity as he hosted a weekly reality show of the Forbidden Zone, from the comfort of his office deep in the Safe Zone.

With Daniel Hildebrande out of the picture, many would think that Tommy would worry. However, he was supremely confident, not just in his own abilities, but in the stupidity of others that he could continue to ascend in power, wealth, and fame. The men who ran the "science division," where Don worked, were now in power after the coup d'etat. Tommy thought despite inter-bureau rivalries, that he would still be in good shape.

"Eric and that vampiress, Abigail, now have a death warrant on their head. To be killed on sight!" Don roared. "Your show is effectively over."

"But what if we change the show up and have Eric--"

Don now towered in front of Tommy, looming over him. The big man stooped so that their noses touched as he grasped Tommy's collar. Don shook his head with his eyes never leaving Tommy's. "It's over. They are to be killed on sight." Don emphasized each word by poking Tommy in the face with his nose to punctuate each shouted syllable.

"Don't try to intimidate me," Tommy said with a knowing smile as he wiped Don's spittle from his face. "I saw little Eric Hildebrande kick your ass."

Suddenly Tommy was suspended off the floor, held by Don's thick fingers around his throat.

"You think this is a joke," Don raged in his face. Don's harsh and heavy breathing now assaulted Tommy's face.

"You can't do this to me" Tommy choked out a protest but the pressure on his trachea shut off anymore words as well as his breath. He thrashed helplessly for a moment and then blacked out from the obstruction on his carotid artery, cutting off the blood flow to the brain.

***

Slowly, Tommy regained his consciousness on the floor. He painfully sat up noticing that he was alone in the room. A stream of blood had dried that extended from his nose into his white collared shirt and disappeared into his retro red paisley tie. He had a knot on his head and his face and his ribcage hurt with each shaky breath. From his bruised body, he realized that Don had kicked and beat him as his unconscious body lay helpless on the floor after choking him unconscious. The big man was gone.

Tommy swore as he got up and stumbled to his computer. He had work to do.

| 19 |

I still heard sporadic fighting and gunfire far down the mountain behind me long after I left the walled town. The gunfire was sparse and intermittent. I was sure that Josh would have it cleaned up shortly, but each distant pop meant someone was desperately defending themselves and someone else met their bloody end.

That knowledge pushed me to run uphill as fast as I could with the weight of the vampiress on my shoulder. When the shooting stopped, there would be flying gunships searching for Abigail and me. We needed as much distance as possible, but so far there were no drones buzzing around me, and I wanted to keep it that way.

However, I could feel less and less muscular response in her body with each of my strides. Soon she was dead weight.

"Abigail?" I called to her on my shoulder. There was no response to my inquiry, not even a subtle flinch.

"Abigail," still nothing. "Abigail!" I exclaimed as terror gripped my heart in an icy fist as I suddenly feared that she had died. I could no longer feel her ribcage expanding and contracting with her breath.

I set her down on the ground and leaned her against a trunk of a thick tree. She started to fall limply to the side, slipping down the rough bark, so I moved her so that her back rested in the hollows formed by diverging roots. I lightly slapped her cheeks.

"Abigail!"

I feared she was gone. My heart filled with a liquid weight of regret as I looked at the good hearted woman who I had wrongly scorned just last night. My mind flashed through our brief interactions over the past few weeks. I thought of how she was at first a dark figure, blacker than the nightly shadows where she had kept watch over me. What was once cryptic and taboo, became my protector and the protector of the Mountain Warrior tribe who some still saw as the enemy. She became the person who I loved more than life, whether we could ever be romantic or not due to her infection. Now she lay before me helpless on her final gasps, if not dead already. I had failed her.

I was grateful when I heard her lungs rasp a breath, but her breathing was ragged as if each straining gasp was her last breath and then let go as a final sigh of resignation of life.

"Abigail!" I voiced again as if pleading for her spirit to remain in her body.

Her eyes fluttered open, and she smiled bravely but weakly at me. The smile was the relief one feels when they fully accept their final fate. I saw her looming death as a soul rendering wound to me. She saw her death as simply letting go of the pain in the world.

"Are you OK?" I asked

She could not hold her head up and looked up at me with eyes rolled up from under her brows.

"No. I am dying. My life… is in minutes… if that."

She gasped for breath a few times after the effort of speaking.

"No no no!" I said as I lightly slapped her as her eyes closed for what I feared was the final time.

Her eyes opened unfocused for a moment. Despite the gray lifeless pallor of her face, her eyes momentarily blazed with the last spark of vampiric life as they finally focused on me. I brushed her thick silky hair away from her face to fully look at her.

"Eric," she said. "I have always loved you."

I hugged her trying to warm her cold body that matched the freezing winter air of the Appalachian Mountains. Her head fell on my shoulder, mouth inches from my throat. I remembered that she had kissed me there not too long ago when she could have bitten me, when she had been ordered to bite me under the threat of death.

"I have always loved you too, but don't say it as a finality," I replied. "How can I help you?"

"You can do nothing for me," she said.

"What do you need?" I asked.

Her eyes rolled up under heavy brows to look into mine. Our faces were inches from each other. The condensation from our breath mixed in the freezing air. She couldn't lift her head. Even rolling her eyes to look at me seemed to tax her reserves, but she didn't say anything.

"What?" I pressed.

"Blood," and she gasped for air after the effort of saying that single word.

"I have blood," I said, letting her head fall into the crook of my shoulder and neck so she could bite my throat.

"Never," she whispered into my neck causing a slight tickle from her breath.

"Do it!" I said into her ear as my hand ran through her hair and I pushed the back of her head to force her mouth on my exposed throat.

"No."

I felt a spark of panic and hopeless anger. I pulled her from the tree and laid her on her back on the ground facing the stars above.

I drew my knife and slit a small section of my wrist, careful to avoid the tendons.

She saw what I was doing.

"No, Eric. Don't. Let me die. I do not wish to… to live like this anymore." It was a lot of words for her breathless state, but she wanted to get her point across. At present, it took as much effort to say that as it did when she threw the nail at the soldier. I feared it was her final reserves.

The blood ran down my hand and onto my fingers. A drop touched her lips and that hunger flashed in her eyes and her nostrils flared at the blood scent. Briefly she looked monstrous.

She whispered in a harsh but quiet rasp, "Don't let your fingers touch my lips, not my teeth. Don't risk infection."

But she was drinking as my blood dripped and then flowed steadily.

I pulled my hand back a little and watched the blood flow into her slack but open mouth. Her eyes brightened with life that slowly spread across her facial features, restoring slight color and muscle powers of expression. She made eye contact with me and I could see her overcome with slight shame and embarrassment. I didn't want her to feel that way, but it gave me hope that her strength and reasoning were returning.

"I love you, too. Now drink. Don't feel shame. I love you," I said.

She drank and even in the starlight, I could see even more color returning to her face.

"I don't know how we will... but we will--" I couldn't finish, but I nodded at her.

I was surprised how quickly she responded to my blood. After a minute, she sat up weakly with her own restored power. Her fiery and hungry eyes were still on the self-inflicted wound on my wrist. I started to yank my arm away. I was well aware of what she was and what the vampiric instinct compelled. Just minutes ago, I had offered her my throat in my passion to save her. Now with her life slowly returning to her, my logic and my instinct for self preservation returned to me. Even she had warned me about being alone with her, especially at night. Especially when consumed with the bloodlust. She was alive but in desperate need of more blood.

"Thank you, Eric. I am in control. Them draining me of my blood has given me total control over my cravings. However, I need more blood, but not yours," she said as she stiffly fully sat up.

She gently took my arm and cleaned the blood off of my hand with a small handkerchief from a pocket in her cloak. Then she looked over my wrist and said, "You cut much deeper than necessary." Despite the hunger for blood in her eyes that blazed with the energy of a madwoman, there was nothing but compassion in her voice and facial expression.

"Feeding vampires is all new to me," I said.

She ignored my dry attempt at humor as she removed a small pouch from her cloak and then placed some powder from the pouch into my wound. I later learned that it was a mix of finely ground herbs designed to stop the bleeding. One herb that I remembered was yarrow. It was supposedly Achilles's magic herb from Greek mythology that stopped bleeding and gave him near immortality on the battlefield. In scientific nomenclature it was even named after him, *Achillea Millefolium.* Then she gave me a cloth and had me place direct pressure on my self-inflicted wound. My blood slowed in its flow as if by a miracle. She quickly wrapped a rag around the wound and tied it like a bandage.

After she finished, I looked at her suspiciously and demanded, "If not my blood, then whose?" Despite giving her my blood, there was no way I would let her take someone else's.

"The blood from that deer," she whispered gently. She then made a quiet shushing sound at me.

I looked in the direction that her nose pointed and saw an innocently young deer walking toward us slowly as if hypnotized. Its gait was fluid, not the halting steps that the cautious animals take as usual when they constantly stop to look around for predators.

She said to me softly, "Don't make any sudden moves. You will break my spell and scare it. I still have my power over the animals of the forest, but it's limited."

I nodded as I watched her black figure slowly and weakly stand to full height. Although her color had returned somewhat, she only lost her monstrous appearance, but instead had an appearance of a recently dead mortal with blazing eyes.

The deer stopped and stared dumbly at her. Despite having offered her my bare neck for blood, I felt unnerved by what I was about to witness. Revulsion overcame me and I felt more akin to the deer than to the vampiress as I realized that I too had once been under her spell, but she had let me live. I tried to convince myself that she had not attempted to place me under her influence in quite some time other than the mind meld when I wanted to kiss her.

I instinctively placed another cloth over my wound to further stem my blood flow just in case, as I watched her, but realized that her poultice had worked. The blood flow had completely halted. Still, I held my wound.

As Abigail walked toward her victim, her eyes focused on the wide dark eyes of the deer. Her hand lithely slid to her waist under her cloak and drew a long slim knife. I couldn't see well in the dark but I found out later that it was a dagger, thinner than my pinkie finger. It had two razor sharp blades on either side and a needle sharp point. Most intelligent vampires preferred to drain their victims of blood with a knife, and drink the blood from a ritualistic chalice. A bite was considered uncivilized, and even worse, sometimes the victim would survive the bite and return for vengeance upon the vampire as another vampire, as in the case of Dexter. However, usually the victims became drooling imbeciles or raging bloodmad psychopaths that were as senseless as zombies.

Some of the intelligent vamps like David, who I had killed last night, just preferred biting their victims because they were sick in the head with a perverse love of dealing death and relished feeling the weakening struggles of their victims as they slowly succumbed and died in their grip. Either way, I despised the vampiric need for blood whether from dagger or bite. As much as I loved Abigail, I wondered if I would ever get over that.

I watched as Abigail strode forward in a relaxed manner as if greeting a pet. As she stepped within a couple feet, she raised the dagger. Despite having just professed my love for her, I was overwhelmed with the urge to scream at the deer, to tell it to run, to avoid its hideous fate, but I couldn't. I wondered for a moment if I had shared the deer's hypnotized blank eyed state when Abigail had approached me in the past.

I could feel my face frown deeply as I watched her plunge the blade into the deer's neck with the skill of a surgeon. The deer's head jerked up. She caressed its neck and whispered reassuringly into its ear. Her voice sounded like a softly spoken lullaby. The animal calmed and looked around as if on guard against predators, unaware of the vampiress at its throat. Its eyes landed suspiciously on me as if I was the one after its blood.

She withdrew the blade and pressed her lips to the wound as the blood spurted out of the small incision. She sucked hungrily, oblivious as I watched in utter disbelief, seeing the trust that the deer had for its parasite.

She quickly regained her healthy glow. When she looked satisfied, she placed her finger over the deer's throat to staunch the flow of blood. She looked at me with a smear of blood around her lips and a few drops dripping down to her chin. She wiped it up with a finger and sucked it off.

"Do you want to keep the deer?" she asked.

"What?" I asked as if in a daze after seeing what I witnessed. I had to admit that it was far more civilized than I expected. I had watched the Mountain Warriors gut and cut up a deer, and I grudgingly admitted that her way was much kinder. I felt more like the savage barbarian, now, compared to her.

"Would you like to take the deer to the village? For food?" she asked.

I still stared at her.

"It will walk with us under my power so that you won't have to carry it. You can kill it as you enter your village," she said. "I know that they are hungry."

I knew I was standing there with my mouth hanging open. The thought of the deer walking like an animated corpse chilled me. I didn't know how to process this.

"Will it live? Uninfected? If you let it go now?" I managed to ask, fearing it might infect the whole tribe.

She nodded. "The vampiric virus only infects humans, and maybe predatory animals."

"Let it go," I said. Although I had grown to really love venison in my short time here, I didn't want that one

Abigail still looked weak, but she was definitely on the way to recovering. However, she saw the state of revulsion on my face. She looked at me with sadness. "You don't want it because you are disgusted with me."

I wanted to deny it to make her feel better, but I felt insane as my mind was in turmoil from the conflicting and simultaneous feelings of intense love for her as a woman and revulsion for this aspect of her. Despite never being able to be intimate with her, I really adored her. It was one thing to see her helpless, but now to see her, a vampire, return to nearly full power, I instinctively questioned my judgment and sanity. I pushed that from my mind and tried to turn my reaction around.

"I mean, I just thought it might turn into a vamp if it lives?"

"No! " she said and smiled, perhaps thinking she had just misunderstood me. " I already told you, this virus only infects people and possibly carnivorous animals," she said.

I nodded, suddenly remembering that she had said that. Mental and physical exhaustion weighed heavily on me. I then thought for a moment before saying, "Let it go, please. I have seen enough death for the evening." I meant that.

She smiled and reached into her pocket and rubbed the same powder into the deer's throat with the same kind tenderness that she applied to my wound on the wrist. She patted the deer on the head then stroked its neck and shoulders with kindness. She then spoke softly into its ear. The deer took a few slow steps away and then looked at both of us with confusion and then with a great bounding leap, it ran into the darkness of the forest.

When I could no longer hear its thundering gallop, I asked, "What did you rub on our wounds?"

"It's an herbal concoction that I made. I am, or was, a certified herbalist," she said with a hint of pride and regret for who she once was.

"You are still a healer," I said, warming back up to her. The initial shock of watching a vampire feed had worn off and I felt my fondness for her return especially after seeing the mercy she gave to the beautiful forest animal.

"Maybe so, but certificates mean very little these days," she said.

"True, but you are still a healer," I repeated. "Don't forget that."

She nodded and looked around as if for a cue card for a conversation direction away from the uncomfortable reality of what just happened.

She finally said, "I can walk on my own now. So…"

She stopped talking and just looked at me. I cocked my head at her.

She asked, "So… Do we go our separate ways now?"

A knife seemed to stab my heart as the reality dawned on me.

"No. No. We stick together," I said. I blurted that without thinking, but those words were my deepest thoughts and longings.

She asked, "Where do we go then? I obviously can not return to the Caverns, but I really need to rest to recuperate for a few days or so. My ribs are still mending and I am not quite me after being drained of blood. I'm a sitting duck in these woods."

I thought for a moment and asked, "You can walk, but are you alright?"

"I can walk for a few miles, but I need to hole up in a safe place and rest for a few days. I may be on my feet now, but I am still very weak. I won't be much use in a fight."

She said that and slowly made her way to the ground in an upright sitting position, too tired to stand. I could see exhaustion and slight pain on her face as she still favored her ribcage where she attained the rib fractures. With the draining of her blood, the healing had halted, but I was glad to see that she didn't have to lean on anything. She now held her head upright, aristocratically, like the rest of her coven and without effort.

"Maybe we can--" she started to say but paused hesitantly in her thoughts.

"What?" I asked.

"I fear other vampires, more than people," she said.

"Me too," I said, trying to be funny and quickly added, "Other than you of course."

"Would the Mountain Warriors let me rest for a few days in their camp? If they let me stay, I would be a great night guard and I can lure wild game."

"Of course," I said without thinking. "We'll get there at night. I can sneak you in my hootch and you can sleep through the day. I will just keep you hidden until we can leave together. They owe you their lives."

"Why should you sneak me in? I saved Bryan's son? They like me, right." She said this with eyes wide in pleading innocence.

At that moment, my heart broke. They always called me naive. She didn't hear Adam threaten to banish me if any more vampires came to visit me, let alone if I invited one into the tribe. I couldn't think of anything to say as she looked at me with growing worry. I finally blurted out, "I need to assure them first that you won't attack anyone."

She glared at me like she would stand up and give me a slap across the face. I felt like I deserved it.

I quickly said, "I know that you won't, but I have to give my word to Bryan. They are terrified of vampires."

"This shit is stupid!" she said.

I had never heard her curse and I knew I was pushing it. I sat down next to her as she glowered at me and I said to her, "I am saying this because when I first came here, I thought it was mankind against zombies and vampires. They still see it that way."

"So what are you saying? There is nothing I can do to earn their trust? I'm an eternal outcast? Why did you even bother to save me?"

"Because you mean the world to me." I said as I placed my hand on her shoulder.

She nodded and said, "Do you still see it as mankind against vampires?"

"No. I see it as us against anyone who would harm us, and I think the best thing to do would be to sneak you in, let you rest up in safety, and when you are strong, we'll go from there. They may let you stay. I don't know, but we'll make something work, but getting you to my tent, where you can regain your strength in the safety of the tribe is the best idea for now."

As I said that, I thought of the bad blood that I had stirred with my attack on Adam, but it was the only place to go while she was weak, with The Specter out for our blood. After all the hands had been played out in Craigsville, the search for Abigail and me would be relentless. Hiding a vampire in the Mountain Warriors tribe was the best option in a series of bad ones.

"We'll make it," I said reassuringly as I gripped her shoulder with the passion of my words.

She looked me deep in the eyes. The intensity unnerved me.

"What?" I asked worriedly.

She said, "David still affects you."

I realized I still heard his whispered chant to kill. She placed her hand on my head and it ceased completely. I felt like the weight of the world lifted from my shoulders and that I saw the world through clear eyes.

"Thanks," I said. "For everything."

Although I had some reservations about her dietary needs, I had the complete awareness that she was my truest friend in all my life as I saw the sincerity in her starlit eyes, and she smiled back when she saw the sincerity in my own.

"Should we go now?" I asked, still sitting beside her.

"Not yet," she said. Her voice still slightly strained with exhaustion. "May I lean and rest on you for a moment?"

We looked deep into each other's eyes.

"Of course," I said, as I opened my arm to her.

Instead of hitting the trail, she leaned into me, and we just held onto each other with affection for quite some time. She leaned her head on my shoulder and I rested my head on her silky hair. We both really needed that. I never wanted to let go of that embrace or her.

ABOUT THE AUTHOR

R.J. Burle is a former Marine and volunteer firefighter. He has studied and taught a variety of martial arts and is an outdoor survival skills instructor. He is a chiropractor and writer living in the mountains near Asheville, NC with his wife and children. This is the fifth book in The Mountain Warriors series. You can find the previous books, *Outcast, Deadly Ally, March of the Dead*, and *Beneath the Caverns* online and through your favorite bookstore. Visit him online at www.rjburle.com and subscribe to his YouTube channel at "R.J. Burle" where you'll find readings of his short stories and book excerpts.

www.ingramcontent.com/pod-product-compliance
Lightning Source LLC
LaVergne TN
LVHW041906070526
838199LV00051BA/2524